# Spirit Quest

By

Vernon Williams

Cover design by Katie Kamara

Soma Fusion Media LLC
3811 Suitland Rd SE
Washington. D.C. 20020
USA

somafusionmedia@gmail.com
www.somafusionmedia.com



Published by Soma Fusion Media LLC 2020

ISBN: (Digital) 978-1-63760-898-2
       (Print) 978-1-63760-899-9

# Acknowledgements

I would like to thank

Katie Kamara

&

Soma Fusion Media LLC

for making this book a reality.

This is a story about five children that have a very magical family. They are Apache and learn the Apache way. Their family taught them if they ask the Creator, they could be anything they wanted to be, but it had to be connected to a sacred site...a holy site. They knew right away where this place had to be... Mt. Graham. They heard about this place from their parents. They had learned a lot from their grandmothers, Mountain Flower and Little Butterfly. They spent a lot of time around their uncle, Spirit Eagle, he taught them the way of the Apache people.

"I want to go to Mount Graham," said Lone Wolf.

"I want to also," said Little Eagle.

"What about the rest of you," asked Lone Wolf

"I want to go," said Spirit Pony.

"Count me in. What about you Sacred Wolf," said Spirit Wolf

"I don't know, that is a long walk," said Sacred Wolf.

"We need you to go. It will take all of us," said Lone Wolf.

"Yeah, come on," said Little Eagle.

"You know you want to, "said Spirit Pony.

"Oh, okay. I better not get dirty," said Sacred Wolf.

"It will be a long walk. We will need supplies," said Lone Wolf.

"I knew this was a bad idea," said Sacred Wolf.

"It's not that bad," said Little Eagle.

"I don't like wearing pants," said Sacred Wolf.

"Look everyone there's a herd of ponies," said Spirit Pony.

"They are beautiful," said Spirit Wolf.

"You think they will let us ride them to Mount Graham?" said Little Eagle

"I will ask them if they will give us a ride," said Spirit Pony.

"Hello, Spirit Pony," said one of the painted ponies.

"You spoke to me with your mind and you know my name. I cannot believe we can speak to each other," Spirit Pony replied.

"How else would I speak to you, I cannot talk any other way, only special people can hear me," said the white and brown pony.

"Will you give us a ride to Mount Graham?" asked Spirit Pony.

"That is what I am here for," said the pony.

"Who sent you?" asked Spirit Pony.

"You ask for me with your mind, so here I am," said the pony.

"I was thinking you must heard me," said Spirit Pony.

"I have been waiting for you to call on me," said the pony.

"You know my name, what is yours," said Spirit Pony.

"My name is Shadow," replied the black horse proudly.

Spirit Pony turned to the others, "Hey, he can talk his name is Shadow, he says he will take us to Mount Graham." Said Spirit Pony.

"How did you speak to the pony?" asked Little Eagle.

"With my mind, all of us can do it, remember we all have special abilities and one of them is speaking to animals with our mind," said Spirit Pony.

"What about saddles and bridles," said Spirit Wolf.

"We will need to talk with mom and dad," said Lone Wolf.

"Let's go, I will ask them," said Little Eagle.

"This day keeps getting worse," said Sacred Wolf.

They headed toward the house, all excited.

"Mom, dad I need to ask you something," said Little Eagle.

"Let me guess, some ponies showed up from nowhere," said Spirit Hawk.

"How did you know Mom," said Lone Wolf.

"Lucky guess," said Spirit Hawk.

"Okay, I have another question," said Little Eagle.

"You need saddles and bridles," said Little Wolf.

"How do you do that Dad, you have got to teach me how," said Little Eagle.

"Someday son, you will learn how," said Little Wolf.

"That would be to cool," said Little Eagle.

"Look in the shed out back," said Little Wolf.

"Let me guess, you knew we were going to need them," said Little Eagle.

"You could say that," said Little Wolf.

"I can't wait to tell everyone, they are going to be so surprised," said Little Eagle.

"If you need anything else, let me know," said Little Wolf.

"Thanks dad, see you in a few," said Little Eagle.

"Anytime son," said Little Wolf.

Little Eagle stepped out onto the porch and point to the shed.

"Hey everybody, Dad said everything we need for the ponies are in the shed behind the house," said Little Eagle.

"Let's go see," said Lone Wolf.

"Wow, there are saddles, bridals, and even blankets," said Spirit Wolf.

"Mom and dad thought of everything," said Spirit Pony.

"Everything except a car to take us," said Sacred Wolf

"Where is your adventure in nature?" asked Little Eagle.

"If I want an adventure with nature I will look in a book or on the computer," said Sacred Wolf.

"You take all the fun out of an adventure trip," said Little Eagle'

"It's not the animals and nature I have a problem with, it's the bugs and dirt," said Sacred Wolf.

Ignoring is sister Lone Wolf stood proud.

" We leave in the morning," said Lone Wolf.

"Yeah," said Little Eagle

"Oh great," said Sacred Wolf.

"I think it's going to be a wonderful adventure, I can't wait," said Spirit Pony.

"I agree with you, we are going to have a lot of fun," said Spirit Wolf.

"It's settled then, we leave in the morning," said Lone Wolf.

They spend the rest of the day preparing the painted ponies for the journey. After dinner, they went to bed early, excited about their first adventure on their own. All they could think about was the trip ahead, all except for Sacred Wolf she tossed and turned most of the night, leaving the rest of the children lying awake.

$$*****$$

The next morning, they ate breakfast, saddled the ponies, and headed to Mount Graham. They could not believe their luck; getting to ride the ponies and not having to walk. The ride to Mt. Graham would take only a few hours. They headed toward the sacred mountain, excited of what the day would bring.

By the time they reached the half waypoint, Lone Wolf saw a pack of wolf's following them.

"Look everyone, a pack of wolves," said Lone Wolf.

"Where? Now we are in for it," said Sacred Wolf.

"I don't think so. I sense they mean us no harm," said Spirit Wolf.

"I sense the same thing. They are here to protect us," said Lone Wolf.

"Is that an eagle I hear," said Spirit Pony.

"It's circling above us," said Little Eagle.

"Can you sense what it is saying," said Lone Wolf.

"Yes, it is telling me to follow him, it is not much further, "said Little Eagle.

"How is everyone hearing these animals when I don't hear a thing," said Sacred Wolf.

"You have to concentrate on the wolves," said Lone Wolf.

"I am trying, I still cannot hear anything," said Sacred Wolf.

"You have to clear your mind, try closing your eyes, then think about the wolves only," said Spirit Pony.

"Okay, I think I hear them," said Sacred Wolf.

"It will get easier if you practice some," said Spirit Wolf.

"Let's follow the eagle," said Little Eagle.'

They arrived at Mount Graham and thanked the ponies for the ride by patting them on the side. Then they thanked the wolves and eagle for their help by waving in their direction. They sent them on their way to find food and water, for they had to be hungry after the long journey.

"This is a beautiful place, "said Spirit Wolf.

"Yes, it is beautiful and remember how sacred it is, "said Sacred Wolf.

'What do we ask the Creator for, "ask Lone Wolf?

"I have all kind of wishes I want, "said Little Eagle.

"I know what I want to ask for, "said Spirit Pony.

"What is that, "said Sacred Wolf.

"I love ponies more than anything, so I would like to be a pony at any time I wish to be, "said Spirit Pony.

"That would be awesome to be an animal any time you want. Do you think the Creator will grant us our wishes, "asked Spirit Wolf.

They agreed that would be the neatest wish ever. They remembered what Grandmother Mountain Flower told them about blessing the four sacred directions starting with the east. After blessing the four sacred directions, they faced the east and said to the Creator:

They each closed their eyes and made their wish "I wish to be my favorite animal."

Then they heard a voice and they realized it was the Creator speaking to them.

*" I will grant you this wish, but there is one condition; you can only use it for good, if it's used for anything other than good, you will lose the ability forever. Do all of you agree?" asked the Creator.*

"Yes," said all the children.

*"Then close your eyes again, hold hands, and make your wish," said the Creator.*

The children squeezed their hands as tight as they could and whispered their wishes.

When they opened their eyes, they all were the animal they wish to be, and the voice of the Creator was gone. Spirit Pony was a beautiful gray pony with a black tail and mane. Little Eagle could not believe he had what look like a twelve foot wingspan, and he was a mighty eagle. Spirit Wolf, Sacred Wolf, and Lone Wolf were three of the bravest looking wolves with dark around the face with spots of white in their gray mane.

"We are our favorite animal," said Little Eagle.

"We can also hear each other's thoughts," said Lone Wolf.

"I never thought I would be able to run so fast, "said Spirit Pony.

"I have never smelled so many different odors in my life," said Lone Wolf.

"Neither have I, "said Spirit Wolf.

"Some of them don't smell so great, "said Sacred Wolf.

"Look, I can fly, *whoa* I almost hit that cactus, I need a little more practice; looks like, "said Little Eagle.

"Practice isn't going to help you see something as big as a cactus, "said Spirit Wolf.

"I can see for miles, it's my wings I have to get control of, "said Little Eagle.

Everyone was having so much fun playing, with exception of Sacred Wolf, who was not about to get dirty rolling around on the ground. Suddenly Sacred Wolf smelled something in the air.

"Hey guys, I think I smell smoke, "said Sacred Wolf.

Everyone stopped and sniffed the air.

"You are right Sacred Wolf, "said Lone Wolf.

"I smell it to, "said Spirit Wolf.

"I will see what I can spot from the air, "said Little Eagle.

"That is a good idea, "said Spirit Pony.

"Don't fly into any moving cactuses, "said Spirit Wolf.

"Don't step on any scorpions, "said Little Eagle.

"Scorpions, is he serious, I hate scorpions, "said Sacred Wolf.

"We live in Arizona, there are all kinds of scorpions here, "said Spirit Pony.

"Don't say that, now I will have to worry, I have no shoes, "said Sacred Wolf.

"Little Eagle is coming back, "said Lone Wolf.

"What did you see, "asked Spirit pony?

"It does not look good, the other side of the mountain is completely on fire, "said Little Eagle.

"What are we going to do," said Sacred Wolf?

"First do not panic, we need to let the Geronimo Hot Shots know, so they can save the mountain, "said Spirit Pony.

"I think they already know, I seen people fighting the fire, "said Little Eagle.

"That is good, the mountain has to be saved, so let's head home, there's nothing we can do now, "said Lone Wolf.

"That's a good ideal," said Sacred Wolf.

"We have bigger problems, "said Little Eagle.

"What is wrong, "asked Lone Wolf?

"There are three children against the side of the mountain trying to get away from the fire, "said Little Eagle.

"Somehow we need to get word to the Hot Shots, "said Spirit pony.

"It is too late; the fire has almost surrounded them. The only way in is from our side," said Little Eagle.

'What are you saying, we have to rescue them, "said Sacred Wolf.

"We have no choice, if we don't, they will not survive. The fire is closing in on them fast, "said Little Eagle.

"You are right; we can do this, "said Lone Wolf.

"Are you crazy, we have no experience in recusing someone, "said Sacred Wolf.

"Are you afraid to get dirty, "asked Spirit Wolf.

"Maybe, I hate the smell of smoke, "said Sacred Wolf.

"We need to go, we don't have time for this, follow me, "said Little Eagle.

"Everyone, help keep an eye on Little Eagle in case I lose sight of him in all the smoke, "said Lone Wolf.

They made their way around the mountain. They could not believe the size of the fire. Most of the forest on that side was in flames. They saw Little Eagle circling overhead.

"Little Eagle is circling, that must be where the children are," said Spirit Wolf.

"I think you are right," said Sacred Wolf.

"There they are, "said Lone Wolf.

Lone Wolf, Spirit Wolf, and Sacred Wolf made their way to the children. When the children saw them, they began to panic, trying to climb the mountainside. Spirit Pony ran in between the children and the wolf pack and told them.

"You need to back off, you are scaring them, "said Spirit Pony.

"Sorry, we forgot that we are a pack of wolves which would scare children, "said Lone Wolf.

"I will get them to climb on my back, "said Spirit Pony.

Spirit Pony stood below them shaking her head and making noise trying to get their attention.

The children noticed the pony through the smoke.

"Look, it is a pony, it is so pretty," said Claire.

"She is kneeling on one knee, "said Tony.

"I think it wants us to get on, "said Randy.

"She does want us to get on, she wants to help," said Claire.

"How do you know it is a girl pony," said Tony.

"I just know because she is so beautiful," said Claire.

"Let's go, the fire is getting closer," said Randy.

They got on the back of Spirit Pony. Clare was first, then Tony and Randy followed.

"I will put Claire in front so I can hang on to her and you ride behind me Randy," said Tony.

"Okay," said Randy.

Spirit Pony made her way to her feet after the children climbed on her back.

"I have them, let's go," said Spirit Pony.

"The smoke is getting to thick to see, I am not sure which way to go," said Lone Wolf.

"What are we going to do," said Spirit Wolf.

"I remember seeing a small river on the way here," said Lone Wolf.

"It is this way, follow me, "said Little Eagle.

"We need to get out of here the children are starting to choke on the smoke," said Spirit Pony.

"This way," said Lone Wolf.

As they made their way through the smoke, it started to get thicker. Spirit Wolf was behind Lone Wolf and the smoke started to burn her eyes making it hard to see where to go. Spirit Wolf stopped and closed her eyes trying to focus. As she opened her eyes, she realized Lone Wolf was no longer in sight; panic consumed her.

Spirit Wolf let out a loud howl praying it would alert Lone Wolf.

Lone Wolf paused and realized he left the others behind. As he glanced back the fire cut off their path.

"I cannot see you no longer, where are you Lone Wolf," said Spirit Wolf.

"Are we lost? Which way do we go," said Sacred Wolf.

"The children cannot take much more of the smoke, we need to find a way out," said Spirit Pony.

"I am trying to figure out which way to go," said Spirit Wolf.

"Listen, I hear something," said Sacred Wolf.

"I hear it also," said Spirit Pony.

"I hear it to and it sounds like Lone Wolf howling back to us; it is coming from this direction, follow me," said Spirit Wolf.

"Don't run off and leave us, I am afraid," said Sacred Wolf.

"Do not worry, I want, now let's go," said Spirit Wolf.

"I can hear Lone Wolf clearer, we must be getting close," said Sacred Wolf.

"We are getting closer, I can also hear him better," said Spirit Pony,

"Keep howling Lone Wolf, we are almost there," said Spirit Wolf.

"I think I see him," said Sacred Wolf.

"There he is," said Spirit Wolf.

"I am glad you finally made it, the fires almost on us," said Lone Wolf.

"There is no way to go except to cross the river," said Spirit Pony.

"This is the only way out," said Lone Wolf.

"It looks like a twenty foot drop," said Spirit Wolf.

"It is that high or higher," said Lone Wolf.

"I will go first," said Spirit Pony.

"No! Sacred Wolf needs to go first, said Lone Wolf.

"You cannot be serious, there is no way I am going to jump in that dirty water and have myself smelling like a wet dog," said Sacred Wolf.

"You have to, it's our only way to get away from the fire," said Lone Wolf.

Spirit Pony kneeled to one knee to let the children off. At the same time, Sacred Wolf looked over the edge at the river, talking to herself. Lone Wolf took advantage of the moment, he sneaks around behind Sacred Wolf, and gives her a push.

"AAAWW, SPLASH. I cannot believe you push me into this dirty water. I will get you Lone Wolf.," said Sacred Wolf.

"You will thank me later," said Lone Wolf.

Tony and Randy jumped off Spirit pony, turning to their sister they said.

"I think she wants us to get off now," said Randy.

"Go ahead I will get Claire, come on Claire, let go of her mane, you have to get off," said Tony.

"No, I don't want to. I am afraid," said Claire.

"You have to, we will help you so don't be afraid," said Tony.

"No, I don't want to, I can't swim," said Claire.

Spirit Pony stood to her feet, shook her head, backed up a few feet, ran and leaped into the river.

"Hang on tight Claire," said Randy.

"SPLASH"

Spirit Pony and Claire went under water a few seconds; Claire was still on Spirit Pony's back when they surfaced. Claire was laughing, and said this is fun.

"Look, I can swim, come on guys this is fun," said Claire.

"I can't believe she stayed on," said Randy.

"I can't believe she likes it," said Tony.

"The last one in, is a rotten egg," said Randy.

"Hey, wait for me," said Tony.

Lone Wolf and Spirit Wolf looked at each other with disbelief, and leaped into the water.

"This water is cold," said Spirit Wolf.

"It fills great," said Lone Wolf.

Down the river a way, Little Eagle was on the other side of the river trying to get Sacred Wolf's attention.

"Over here, "said Little Eagle

"I'm trying! You know I cannot swim very well, "said Sacred Wolf.

"Swim! Swim, "said Little Wolf.

"Finally, I made it to shore, said Sacred Wolf.

"I would give you a hand, but as you can see I don't have one, said Little Eagle."

"You're lucky; you don't have to swim, "said Sacred Wolf.

"You're telling me, that water looks pretty dirty," said Little Wolf.

"Look at me, I am a mess and I stink like a wet dog," said Sacred Wolf.

"Look there's the children and Spirit Pony," said Little Eagle.

"That was fun, I want to do it again," said Claire.

"Forget that, I want a shower," said Sacred Wolf.

"Claire! Are you okay, "asked Tony.

"Did you see me, I was swimming," said Claire.

"We saw that," said Randy.

"We told you if you tried you could swim," said Tony.

"You did really well," said Randy.

"Not without the pony's help, I love you pony," said Claire

"Look, there's Lone Wolf and Spirit Wolf," said Little Eagle.

"That was refreshing," said Lone Wolf.

"If you don't mind getting dirty and smelling like a wet dog," said Sacred Wolf.

"I don't smell like a dog," said Spirit Pony.

"I don't either," said Little Eagle.

"Don't think I forgot how I got wet Lone Wolf," said Sacred Wolf.

"I don't know what you're talking about, was only trying to help," said Lone Wolf.

"We need to get on moving. I am sure the kid's parents are worried and I know the children are hungry," said Spirit Pony.

"They're not the only one hungry," said Little Eagle.

"I need to shake some of this water off first," said Lone wolf.

"Me to," said Spirit Wolf.

"Thanks a lot you two, now I really do smell bad," said Sacred Wolf.

"No problem," said lone wolf.

"Do you believe this, my feet are covered with dirt," said Sacred Wolf.

"Looks like they are ready to go, the pony is kneeling for use to get on," said Randy.

"Well, let's go, I can't wait to get home," said Tony.

"Neither can I. I am starving," said Randy.

"I am starting to have fun now. I'm no longer afraid," said Claire.

"Let's go everyone, it's going to be dark soon," said Lone Wolf.

"I'm getting hungry also," said Little Eagle.

"You can eat anytime, whether you're hungry or not, "said Sacred Wolf.

"I want deny that, I love to eat," said Little Eagle

Everyone needs to stop fussing and we need to get going, the children are hungry also," said Spirit Pony.

"Your right Spirit Pony, I can hear their stomach's growling," said Lone Wolf.

"I already scouted the area, we need to head this way," said Little Eagle.

"I can't wait to get home and take a shower," said Sacred Wolf.

"Don't go to fast, I'm afraid the kid's may fall off and get hurt, said Spirit Pony.

"We want. Let's go," said Lone Wolf.

They take off hoping to find help along the way. They did not go far when they came up on some firefighters.

"Look over there Lone Wolf, firefighters." said Spirit Wolf.

"Good, we can give the children to them," said Lone wolf.

"Good idea," said Sacred Wolf.

"What does that mean," said Spirit Pony.

'Just thinking we could get home faster if we leave the children with the firefighters," said Spirit Wolf.

"I can't wait to wash this stink off me," said Sacred Wolf.

Suddenly they heard one of the firefighters say, *look wolves.* One of the firefighters pulls a handgun; in fear, the wolves will attack them. Before he could get a shot off Little Eagle swooped down and knocks the gun out of the firefighter's hand. Before the firefighter can retrieve it, one of the other firefighters grabbed him by his shoulder.

"Look! Wait."

"Where did those children come from," asked firefighter.

"I don't know, it's as if the animals saved the children," said another firefighter.

Spirit Pony came up to the firefighters and kneeled so the children could get down.

"Are you children ok?" asked firefighter.

"We are fine," said Tony.

"I am hungry," said Randy.

"We need to ask you a few questions first, if you don't mind. Where are your parents and how did you get separated," said the firefighter.

"We went on camping trip a few days ago. We went for a walk, not realizing the forest was on fire, by the time we noticed, the fire cut our path off and we could not get back to our parents. Then we decided to make our way to Mount Graham, hoping to find high ground to get away from the fire," said Tony.

"Minutes later these animals showed up to help us," said Randy.

"If it wasn't for them we wouldn't be here now," said Claire.

"That sounds like an amazing story," said the firefighter.

"It's not just a story, it really happen," said Tony.

"We got a call earlier about three children missing, you must be them," said the firefighter.

"That had to be our parents. Where are they," said Tony.

"I will take you to them," said the firefighter.

"Wait! I have to tell my friends bye," said Claire.

"You go right ahead, them are truly some amazing animals," said the firefighter.

"They are more than amazing, they are our friends and they saved our lives," said Randy.

"We have to get going," said the firefighter.

"I have to say goodbye. That was the most fun I ever had. I will miss all of you and I love you, goodbye, goodbye. I love you," said Claire.

They headed out of the smoked filled area. On the way out they talked about their friends and wondered if they would ever see them again.

"I haven't had so much fun in a long time," said Lone Wolf

"Neither have I," said Spirit Wolf.

"Speak for yourself, I have never missed home so much," said Sacred Wolf.

"You may be aggravating, but without you we wouldn't have as much fun," said Little Eagle.

"You call that fun," said Sacred Wolf.

"I hope the children find their parents," said Spirit Pony.

"They will, I heard one of the firefighters say he bet that was the children that was reported missing," said Lone Wolf.

"I hope so," said Spirit Pony.

No one spoke for the rest of the trip, they had so much stuff to tell their parents, and especially how they saved those three kids. Of course, with the exception of Sacred Wolf, the only thoughts on her mind was taking a shower. It was an exciting day but some parts were scary. They walked and walked for hours.

As the sun set the faint image of home surfaced.

"I see the house just ahead," said Little Eagle.

"We need to stop and change back to our human form," said Lone Wolf.

"Can we do that not being at Mount Graham, said Spirit Wolf.

"I'm not sure, we left in such a big hurry I forgot about changing back," said Lone Wolf.

"We have to try anyway, I need a shower," said Sacred Wolf.

"Let's form a circle and think of our human form, see what happens," said Lone Wolf.

They formed the circle and within minutes they were back in human form.

"It worked," said Little Eagle.

"I can't wait to wash this filth off me," said Sacred Wolf.

"I can't wait to eat," said Little Eagle

"Let's go everyone, we are almost home," said Lone Wolf.

"I bet mom and dad will be so shocked when we tell them what happen," said Spirit Pony.

"You know they will be," said Lone Wolf.

"Look there is the house," said Little Eagle.

"I'm going to be the first one in the shower," said Sacred Wolf.

As they stepped upon the porch, they turned the doorknob and stepped inside noticing their parents sitting on the couch.

"Mom, dad, you're not going to believe what we did," said Spirit Pony.

"One minute sweetie we are watching the news," said Spirit Hawk.

On the screen, there was the firefighters that took the children. They all stood and listened to the news reporter.

"We have an amazing story to tell, coming from the smoked filled canyon stated the reporter."

They all watched as the reporter held up a picture of a Hot Shot firefighter showing the image he captured with his cell phone.

The reporter turned to the firefighter and asked. "What happen today out in the smoked filled canyon,"

"I couldn't believe what happen myself, I am glad I had my cell phone with me. There was a pony, an eagle, and three wolves. Here, let the film speak for itself," said the fire fighter.

"That's us," shouted Spirit Pony.

"That is amazing, you guys are on TV," said Little Wolf.

Lone Wolf stared at his dad.

"Dad you already know that we can turn into animals? said Lone Wolf.

"Yes, son we know. Your mother and I have something we need to tell all of you," said Little Wolf.

"What's that dad," said Spirit wolf.

I'll let your mother tell you," said Little Wolf.

"I would rather your father tell you," said Spirit Hawk.

"Children, remember we told you, you could be whatever you wanted to be," said Little Wolf.

"Yeah, dad we remember," said Lone Wolf.

"How do you think you got your native names? We knew what your favorite animal was when you were born," said Little Wolf.

"So, you know what we can do? You know that it's us," said Spirit Pony.

"Yes, we know," said Spirit Hawk.

"Let's watch the rest of it, you're not going to believe what Little Eagle did," said Spirit Wolf.

"I think we already missed it while we were talking," said Lone Wolf.

"That's okay, we recorded it. We seen it earlier, it has been all over the news, said Little Wolf.

'Let's watch it again," said Spirit Pony.

"Wait, let me grab a snack, I'm hungry, said Little Eagle.

"Does everyone want to eat first," said Spirit Hawk.

"Not me, I want to take a shower first, you guys go ahead," said Sacred Wolf.

"She has been saying that all day. She is so afraid of getting dirty," said Spirit Pony.

"Let's watch the news again dad," said Lone Wolf.

"Ok son. You better come on Little Eagle," said Little Wolf.

"I am coming dad," said Little Eagle.

"What do you think is going to happen to Mount Graham dad," said Lone Wolf.

"We are hoping the tree's get replanted and when everyone sees what all you did by helping the children they will see that Mount Graham is truly a sacred place," said Little Wolf.

"Here it goes, watch what Little Eagle does mom and dad," said Lone Wolf.

"Little Eagle, what if you would have got shot when you swooped down and knocked the gun out of the firefighter's hand?"

"Yes, exactly what if someone got hurt or even killed," said Spirit Hawk.

"Oh mom, that why we have Little Eagle.

"Yeah mom, they have me to watch over them," said Little Eagle.

"Your mom and I worry about all of you. We love you," said Little Wolf.

"Okay mom and dad, we will be more careful," said Lone Wolf.

'Look at the teeth on Lone Wolf when that firefighter pulled a gun on them," said Little Eagle.

They all start laughing. The day could have ended in a different way but thanks to the bravery of the animals, everybody survived.

Spirit Hawk looked at her children. She was very proud of them but she also worried about their safety.

"We must speak to the children soon, Little Wolf they must understand that their safety is first and foremost.

Little Wolf smiled, "Yes, we will they are just so excited so let's give them that today. We will speak to them tomorrow."

They watched their children as they sat and watched the news clip over and over. They were very proud of them but they wondered what their next adventure would entail.


A week passed since the children visited Mount Graham. The children were outside playing with exception of Spirit Pony, who stayed inside hanging out with her parents. Spirit Pony goes to enter her parents' bedroom when she hears them talking on the phone. They are talking about a place called Oak Flats. The part of the conversation she could make out was about a mining company wanting to destroy a sacred mountain to extract minerals, which would destroy the sacred site, it would also pollute the land, water and disperse many of the animals and even wipe out some species. Spirit Pony grew furious and could not wait to tell her brothers and sisters. She made her way to the front door and eased it open and stepped out into the warmth of the day.

"Hey everybody, wait till you hear what I heard," said Spirit Pony.

"What's wrong Spirit Pony," said Little Eagle?

"You're not going to believe what I heard mom and dad talking about on the phone," said Spirit Pony.

"You already said that once," said Sacred Wolf.

"Yeah, what's got you so upset," said Spirit Wolf.

"I overheard mom and dad talking to someone on the phone says a mining company wants to destroy a sacred mountain for the minerals," said Spirit Pony.

"They can't do that, we have to stop them somehow," said Lone Wolf.

"I agree with you," said Little Eagle.

"I also agree with you," said Spirit Wolf

"I'm not sure I do," said Sacred Wolf.

"What you mean, you don't agree," said Lone Wolf.

"Yes, I agree, it's all the dirt, not just any dirt, its mining dirt. You will never be able to get it out of your cloths or off your skin," said Sacred Wolf.

"What about the animals, water, land, and the mountain itself," said Spirit Pony.

"I care about all of them, why can't we do it from inside the house on the phone," said Sacred Wolf.

"That's not how it works," said Little Eagle.

"Little Eagles right, we have to go and get evidence and samples," said Lone Wolf.

"Okay, I'm not going to touch anything," said Sacred Wolf.

"We have to tell mom and dad and find out where it is," said Lone Wolf.

"You can't just walk up and ask them, they will know I was ease dropping," said Spirit Pony.

"I have an ideal, follow me," said Spirit Wolf.

They all ran with Spirit Wolf into the house.

"Hi! Mom, dad, have you heard anything about Mount Graham" said Spirit Wolf.

"Yes we have children, why do you ask," said Spirit Hawk.

"We were wondering if anything was being done for the Mountain," said Spirit Wolf.

"Trees are being replanted by the community and the Medicine Man is working on keeping the mountain from being destroyed," said Spirit Hawk.

"Is that the only mountain in danger of being destroyed," said Spirit Wolf.

"Most of our sacred sights are in danger," said Little Wolf.

"Why is that dad," said Spirit Pony.

'We were talking about another mountain in jeopardy of being destroyed, I think you already know that, don't you children," said Little Wolf.

"Why would you say that dad," said Spirit Wolf.

"Let's say a bird told you, or in this case a pony," said Little Wolf.

"You're right mom, dad Spirit Pony overheard you talking on the phone about Oak Flats," said Lone Wolf.

"Lone Wolf you weren't supposed to tell them," said Spirit Pony.

"That's where you are wrong Spirit Pony honesty is the best police, always tell the truth," said Little Wolf.

"So! What is going on at Oak Flats, said Lone Wolf.

"Well son, the mining companies are wanting to mine the mountain by collapsing the mountain in on itself," said Little Eagle.

"That would destroy the entire Mountain, not to mention the water, land animals and anyone living near the mountain," said Lone Wolf.

"We cannot let that happen," said Little Eagle.

"We know son. The Medicine Man is trying to stop it as we speak," said Little Wolf.

"He can't do it on his own, can he," said Lone Wolf.

"I'm not sure son, most of the time it takes the community to pull together to stop something like this," said Little Wolf.

"I think we should go there, take pictures and samples of the water, soil, and anything else we can find," said Lone Wolf.

"That's a good ideal," said Spirit Wolf.

"It's almost a day's ride on horseback," said Little Wolf.

"To bad everyone can't fly like me, "said Little Eagle.

"There's nothing wrong with walking, I'm afraid of heights anyway," said Sacred Wolf.

"We can make a camping trip out of it," said Lone Wolf.

"You can't be serous, that means sleeping on the ground, in the dirt," said Sacred Wolf.

"Would you like to stay home with us," said Spirit Hawk.

'Yes," said Sacred Wolf.

"No! We need you Sacred Wolf, even if you are to girlie, we still love you and need you" said Spirit Pony.

"That's where I take after mom, so it's not my fault, right dad," said Sacred Wolf.

"No I wouldn't change any of my girls or sons ways. I love all of you just the way you are, especially your mom, she carried all of you," said Little Wolf.

"So, are you going," said Spirit Wolf.

"Yes, I'll go. The only reason is to save the mountain and all the animals there and for no other reason," said Sacred Wolf.

"Good! We need to get ready, it's going to be a long walk even for wolves," said Lone Wolf.

"We can ride the ponies. We can get there in half the time," said Spirit Pony.

"Can you get them to come," said Sacred Wolf.

"Of course I can. All I have to do is ask them. They will be here by morning," said Spirit Pony.

"Good, I hate long walks," said Sacred Wolf.

"Now, we have that taken care of we need to get supplies together and get some rest, we have a long ride tomorrow," said Lone Wolf.

"That's a good idea son," said Little Wolf.

"I will put some food together to take with you," said Spirit Hawk.

"I am going to help your mother," said Little Wolf.

"We will get supplies together," said Lone Wolf.

"Hey love, did I since worry from you," said Little Wolf.

"It scares me to know they are alone, they are children. You see what happened last time," said Spirit Hawk.

"Yes, I know, I contacted some friends to help guide them. They will meet them at the camp sight," said Little Wolf.

"You did. Thank you, babes, you know how much I love you. I fill better now," said Spirit Hawk.

"I'll do what it takes to make my love happy," said Little Wolf.

"I need to see what I can find for the children to take with them," said Spirit Hawk.

"Ok! I need to contact my friends and let them know when the children are leaving," said Little Wolf.

"Okay," said Spirit Hawk.

"Hey, they are going to be ok," said Little Wolf.

"I know, It scares me, they are my babies," said Spirit Hawk.

"I fill the same way love, but you know our children are special. They have a strong connection with the earth and all its inhabitances, plants, and animals," said Little Wolf.

"I understand, I worry about them when they take off saving sacred sights, cause there is always trouble with people that want to destroy the land," said Spirit Hawk.

"They will be ok, I promise you," said Little Wolf.

"Hey mom dad, we have everything we need except food. Mom why are you crying," said Lone Wolf.

"It's nothing son, your father gave me some good news, it makes me happy," said Spirit Hawk.

"Ok mom! I am going to the kitchen and pack some food to take with us. Grownups, they cry more than kids," said Lone Wolf.

"Let me give you a hand son," said Spirit Hawk.

"I am going to see if the girls need anything," said Little Wolf.

"Ok dad, mom and I will be in the kitchen if you need us," said Lone Wolf.

"Hi girls, how is it going," said Little Wolf.

"Okay dad, we are almost finished packing," said Spirit Wolf.

"You think your taking enough with you Sacred Wolf," said Little Wolf.

"I want to be prepared for anything that might go wrong," said Sacred Wolf.

"You mean like falling in the water," said Spirit Wolf.

"No! More like getting pushed in by Lone Wolf," said Sacred Wolf.

"Hey, He may have saved your life," said Spirit Pony.

"Alright girls let's try to get along while you're gone. I am going to the kitchen," said Little Wolf.

Little Wolf chuckled as he walked out of the room pausing when he heard them arguing.

"I didn't need no help, I could have threw myself in the river," said Sacred Wolf.

"You sure were taking your time," said Spirit Wolf.

"You thought she would have thanked him," said Spirit Pony.

"For what, getting me dirty," said Sacred Wolf.

Little Wolf resurfaced in the doorway.

"Children listen to me, first I want to know I can see what both of you are trying to say. Sacred Wolf hates getting dirty and I understand her. On the other hand, Lone Wolf thought he was only trying to help because he loves you. The way I look at it is he was only trying to help and the dirt will wash off," said Little Wolf.

"But dad it also stinks," said Sacred Wolf.

"I know Sacred Wolf but, you need to put yourself in Lone Wolf's shoes, you may see he only did it because he loves you and the love of a family always comes first," said Little Wolf.

"Yeah, that's why I did it for the reason dad said," said Lone Wolf.

"I see now why, can you do me a favor, next time let me throw myself in the water," said Sacred Wolf.

"I can do that as long as you do not take all day to decide," said Lone Wolf.

"Okay and I love you to Lone Wolf, all of you," said Sacred Wolf.

"Is all this mushy stuff over, I am ready to eat and go to bed, we will need our rest for tomorrow, " said Little Eagle.

"Little Eagle's right, let's go eat, " said Little Wolf.

"I thought we were never going to eat. The last one to eat may not get any, "said Little Eagle.

"Let's go kids, it's almost dinner time. Do not forget to wash your hands," said Little Wolf.

"Dad, can we talk a minute," said Lone Wolf.

"Sure son, what do you need," said Little Wolf.

"How is mom doing?" said Lone Wolf.

"She is a lot better now, after I had a talk with her," said Little Wolf.

"What was wrong with her," said Lone Wolf.

"You will know when the time comes. Now, let's go eat before Little Eagle eats it all," said Little Wolf.

"Ok dad I'll race you," said Lone Wolf.

"That not fair, you got a head start," said Little Wolf.

They all sat around the dinner table talking and laughing. After dinner, they watched the news and talked about their big adventure until around 9 o'clock.

"Isn't it time for bed?" said mom.

"Yeah we are heading there now. Night, love you both." Said Lone Wolf.

"Night kids, we love you too."

The night ended with a sense of calmness as they all fell to sleep.


*****


The next morning the kids woke up at 5 o'clock looking forward to the trip ahead. They eat breakfast, pack for the trip and prepare to leave.

"You kids finished packing," said Little Wolf.

"I believe so dad," said Lone Wolf.

"I want all of you to follow me to the living room, there is a surprise waiting for you," said Little Wolf.

"Look, its Nana Mountain Flower and Nana Pretty Flower," said Spirit Wolf.

"What brings you here so early Nana's," said Spirit Pony.

"We heard what happen on the last trip you went on," said Nana Pretty Flower.

"We can take care of ourselves, they have me to protect them," said Little Eagle.

"We know you can, that doesn't stop us from worrying about all of you," said Mountain Flower.

"Can you not see by looking at us, we are not babies? That's what daddy said," said Little Eagle.

"Yes I said that son and all of you seem to grow more every day," said Little Wolf.

I know they have grown some since I saw them last," said Pretty Flower.

"Your mom worries about you when you're gone for days. For that reason we made a bracelet for each of you, to protect you from harm," said Mountain Flower.

"Oh Nana, they are beautiful," said Sacred Wolf.

"What do you say to your Nana's," said Little Wolf.

"Thank you Nana's," said everyone at the same time.

"Yes, thank both of you," said Spirit Hawk.

"We better eat so we can head out on our trip," said Lone Wolf.

They sat at the table to eat breakfast and talked about how much they missed their Nanas. They also told the story about the last trip and how much fun they had.

"I am so full, I can hardly walk," said Little Eagle.

"You better worry if you will be able to fly," said Spirit Pony.

"You are right, I never thought about it," said Little Eagle.

"With us having to take extra supplies you may want to consider riding with us," said Lone Wolf.

"Your right, we could have fun on the way," said Little Eagle.

"We best get started packing the horses so we can get moving," said Lone Wolf.

"We can pack the horses, and then tell everyone bye," said Spirit Wolf.

"Someone may have to help me with my things," said Sacred Wolf.

"How much are you taking," said Lone Wolf.

"Enough, I hope," said Sacred Wolf.

"You taking all of that," said Spirit Pony.

"We are only going to be gone for three days," said Little Eagle.

"You will need an extra horse for all that, said Lone Wolf.

"Then you better go get one because I have to have a change of clothes for each day, plus my perfumes and makeup." Said Sacred Wolf.

"Okay, but you sure are a lot of trouble." Said Little Eagle as he headed to the barn to get another horse.

✶✶✶✶✶

They packed the horses and went back in to tell their parents bye.

"We have everything ready to go," said Lone Wolf.

"We want you to keep focused, this trip could get dangerous," said Little Wolf.

"You think so this might be a fun trip after all," said Little Eagle.

"Lets go everyone, we are burning daylight," said Lone Wolf.

"Lone Wolf, come here son," said Spirit Hawk.

"Yes mom, what's wrong you look worried," said Lone Wolf.

"I'm just concerned about everyone's safety. That's why I want to ask you to watch out for the rest and I love all of you with all my heart," said Spirit Hawk.

"I will mom and we love you. We will see you in three days, bye," said Lone Wolf.

"Bye everyone, we'll be back before you know it. We love you," said Spirit Wolf.

"Yes, we will be back soon, I'll see to that. I can't hardly think about stinking for more than three days," said Sacred Wolf.

Let's go, we have a long ride before setting up camp," said Lone Wolf.

"Bye mom, dad, Nans, we love you," said Little Eagle.

"Bye children, be careful and we love you," said Little Wolf.

They stood and watch the children ride out of sight. Prayers were with them for protection on their journey ahead.

*****

The children rode most of the day at a gallop, only stopping to water the horses twice. Evening drew upon them as they reached a hill to camp and the view was breath taking. They learned from their parents to always camp on high grown.

"This is a perfect place to camp for the night," said Lone Wolf.

"Lone Wolf said we will camp on that hill over there," said Little Eagle.

"That's a good place," said Spirit Pony.

"All I want is to get off the pony and change clothes," said Sacred Wolf.

"I can't wait to eat," said Little Eagle.

"Let's go everyone, we need to set up camp before it gets dark," said Lone Wolf.

"The last one to the top of the hill has to gather fire wood," said Little Eagle.

They took off toward the top of the hill. The sound of all the creatures of the night started making their presence known.

"This looks like a good spot to set up camp," said Lone Wolf.

"It looks perfect," said Spirit Wolf.

"I agree, you can see in all directions for miles," said Lone Wolf.

"All I want to see is clean cloths and a sleeping bag to set on," said Sacred Wolf.

"What are you going to do when you go to sleep and all the critters are out crawling all over you," said Little Wolf.

"Oh no, I never even thought about them," said Sacred Wolf.

"I don't want to sleep next to Sacred Wolf, she will be the first one the critters go for," said Spirit Wolf.

"I hate critters. Someone will have to set up all-night to make sure nothing gets on me while I sleep," said Sacred Wolf.

"What about sleep," said Spirit Pony?

"That's not my problem," said Sacred Wolf.

"Everyone needs to relax, first of all, there's hardly any crittera out and we will have a fire which will help keep them away," said Lone Wolf.

"Okay, I feel better now," said Sacred Wolf.

"Well, I was told that fire attracts snakes," said Little Eagle.

"What, you serious, I can't sleep on the ground. No, no way," said Sacred Wolf.

"Okay everybody, that's enough. Can you see your scaring her to death? They are only joking around with you. Right everybody," said Lone Wolf.

"Yes we are," said Spirit Pony.

"We are trying to have fun," said Spirit Wolf.

"It's not funny," said Sacred Wolf.

"The fun is over. I want Spirit Pony and Spirit Wolf to water and feed the horses. Little Eagle and Sacred Wolf gather wood while I start a fire," said Lone Wolf.

"I want to feed the ponies. Let one of them, gather wood." said Sacred Wolf.

"I will help gather wood," said Spirit Wolf'.

"Come on Sacred Wolf I'll protect you," said Spirit Pony.

"I'll get a fire started while you two gather wood, then we'll eat," said Lone Wolf.

"That's the best idea I've heard all day," said Little Eagle.

"Here Little Eagle, I brought a hatchet, you may need it," said Lone Wolf.

"More than likely we will, let's go Spirit Wolf," said Little Eagle.

"Right behind you," said Spirit Wolf.

Where are we going to get food and water for the horses," said Sacred Wolf.

"The boys packed it on one of the horses," said Spirit Pony.

"We have to unpack it," said Sacred Wolf.

"It won't unpack itself," said Spirit Pony.

"This trip is turning out to be more work than fun," said Sacred Wolf.

"The horses can't unpack their self," said Spirit Pony.

"I should have gathered wood, it would have been easier," said Sacred Wolf.

"If you will stop complaining and help, it will go faster," said Spirit Pony.

"What about the saddles," said Sacred Wolf.

"The boys will have to remove them. They are too heavy for us," said Spirit Pony.

"That's good, I was beginning to worry," said Sacred Wolf.

"Okay, I still don't like it," said Sacred Wolf.

"Look at all the wood we found," said Little Eagle.

"Yeah, there's a lot more where this came from," said Spirit Wolf.

"Good we are going to need it with Sacred Wolf with us," said Lone Wolf.

"Isn't that the truth," said Little Eagle.

"She means well," said Lone Wolf.

"I know, she's a little aggravating, but that doesn't mean I don't love her," said Little Eagle.

"Don't forget she is one of us. We may look alike, but we act very different. I wouldn't have any other way," said Spirit Wolf.

"You two gather more fire wood, I'm going to go help the girls remove the saddles off the horses," said Lone Wolf.

"We will have it done by the time you return," said Little Eagle.

"I'll be back in a few minutes," said Lone Wolf.

"Here come's Lone Wolf," said Spirit Pony.

"It's about time," said Sacred Wolf.

"Is everything ok," said Lone Wolf.

"The usually with Sacred Wolf," said Spirit Pony.

"Okay, I understand," said Lone Wolf.

"Why can't you leave the saddles on, so you want have to put them back on tomorrow," said Sacred Wolf.

"The horses can't sleep with the saddles on," said Lone Wolf.

"Lone Wolf is right, Sacred Wolf. Would you sleep in your clothes," said Spirit Pony.

"There's no way I could ever do that," said Sacred Wolf.

"The saddle is the same as your clothes. The horses don't like sleeping with their saddles on," said Spirit Pony.

"It makes sense now I understand, we need to make the horses comfortable," said Sacred Wolf.

"That's why I am here to remove the horse's saddles. You also need to tie a rope from tree to tree and tie the horses up so they don't run off in the middle of the night," said Lone Wolf.

"What do we feed the horses," said Sacred Wolf.

"There is water and oats, use the bags and a water bucket," said Lone Wolf.

"Everything we need is on the packed horse," said Spirit Pony.

"This is the last saddle, if you two have this I'm going to go and start a fire so we can eat dinner," said Lone Wolf.

"Yes, please do I am starving," said Sacred Wolf.

"You're starting to sound like Little Eagle," said Spirit Pony.

"All this work I'm doing, makes me hungry," said Sacred Wolf'.

"I'm going to start a fire now," said Lone Wolf.

"A few more trips, we will have enough wood, said Little Eagle.

"I hope so, I'm starting to get hungry," said Spirit Wolf.

"I have been hungry for a while," said Little Eagle.

"Hey guy's, looks like you're about finished with the wood," said Lone Wolf.

"A couple more trips should do it," said Little Eagle.

"We will be eating in twenty minutes," said Lone Wolf.

"Let's go Little Eagle, I can't wait to eat and rest," said Spirit Wolf.

"We fed the horses, all we have left is to water these last two and we are finished," said Spirit Pony.

"I am more than ready to take a break," said Sacred Wolf.

"I am almost finished," said Spirit Pony.

"I wonder how Spirit Wolf and Little Eagles doing." said Sacred Wolf.

"Let's go find out, we are finished," said Spirit Pony.

"This is the last load of wood," said Little Eagle.

"That should be plenty to last most of the night," said Lone Wolf.

"Hey everybody, we finished feeding the horses," said Spirit Pony.

"Everyone's just in time for dinner," said Lone Wolf.

"I am sure everyone is hungry just like I am," said Little Eagle

"When are you not hungry," said Sacred Wolf.

"I warmed up some left over soup, mom sent with us," said Lone Wolf.

"I'm starving," said Little Eagle.

"Mom's soup is always good," said Spirit Pony.

"Look, someone is coming," said Sacred Wolf.

"It's a spirit, a good spirit," said Spirit Pony.

"How can you tell," said Sacred Wolf.

"There is a white light around him. Looks like a man," said Spirit Pony.

"Is he a friendly spirit," said Sacred Wolf.

"Yes, he is. See how white he is. If he wasn't friendly, he would be a dark spirit," said Spirit Wolf.

"It's still a little scary," said Sacred Wolf.

"Who are you and why are you here," said Lone Wolf.

*"My name is Dark Thunder," said Dark Thunder.*

"That sounds awfully scary," said Sacred Wolf.

*"Don't be afraid Sacred Wolf I come in peace," said Dark Thunder.*

"How do you know my name," said Sacred Wolf.

*"Where I am from, all of you are known by everyone," said Dark Thunder.*

"Why are you here," said Little Eagle.

*"I was asked by your parents to watch over you on your journey," said Dark Thunder.*

"That's what dad meant, I would know when the time was right," said Lone Wolf.

"What are you talking about Lone Wolf," said Spirit Pony.

"Something dad said before we left. At the time I didn't understand, I do now," said Lone Wolf.

"Don't dad think we can handle it on our own," said Little Eagle.

"I think it would be a good idea to have a grown up with us," said Sacred Wolf.

"I think so to and I think dad did it for mom, didn't he," said Spirit Wolf.

"Yes, I walked in on them and mom had been crying," said Lone Wolf.

"Why was she crying," said Spirit Pony.

"It was because on our last journey we ran into trouble and it scared mom," said Lone Wolf.

"Why did they not let us know," said Little Eagle.

"They were afraid we wouldn't go to Oak Flats," said Lone Wolf.

*"That is true. What you children are doing is very important to the survival of the Mother Earth,"* People don't concern *themselves with the pollution of the earth or what we call home,"* said Dark Thunder.

"You are so right when you put it that way DarkThunder. Do you mind if I call you Thunder. You're not dark, actually you are a light color" said Sacred Wolf.

*"No, I do not mind,"* said Dark Thunder.

"We are fixing to eat dinner you are welcome to join us if you like," said Spirit Wolf.

"Can you eat the same food we do," said Spirit Pony.

*"Yes I can. All I have to do is touch whatever I want and it will appear,"* said Dark Thunder.

"That's something I would like to do, instead of having to prepare food," said Lone Wolf.

*"You can also say what you want me to have, you make a check mark and it will appear,"* said Dark Thunder.

"Now, that's what I want to do for myself," said Little Eagle.

*"You cannot do it for yourself or family members, it has to be a friend or someone that has less,"* said Dark Thunder.

"Are you going to be with us on the entire journey Thunder," said Sacred Woolf.

*"I will be with you on every journey you take,"* said Dark Thunder.

"We look forward to you joining us on our journeys," said Lone Wolf.

*"I look forward to it myself, you best get some rest, morning comes early,"* said Dark Thunder.

"He is right, we need to get some sleep," said Lone Wolf."

"Where am I going to sleep?  I cannot sleep on the ground with the bugs," said Sacred Wolf.

"Relax Sacred Wolf, I brought you a fold out cot," said Lone.

"I am so tired it want take a few minutes for me to fall asleep," said Sacred Wolf.

"Good night everyone," said Little Eagle.

"Yeah, good night everyone, good Dark Thunder," said Sacred Wolf.

"Are you going to bed Thunder," said Spirit Pony.

*"Maybe later, I am going to check on the horses, good night children,"* said Dark Thunder.

It did not take the children long to fall asleep, after the hard ride they had earlier that day. Thunder spent the night watching over the children. He has a choice to sleep or not, he chose not to in order to keep his promise to the children's father, that is the Apache way.

＊＊＊＊＊

The next morning the children were startled awake by Thunder.

*"Lone Wolf, wake up, wake up Lone Wolf," said Dark Thunder.*

"What is it Thunder, something wrong," said Lone Wolf.

*"Hurry, wake the other children," said Dark Thunder.*

"What's wrong," said Lone Wolf.

*"I will tell you after everyone is awaken, we have trouble coming," said Dark Thunder.*

"Everybody wake up, wake up," said Lone Wolf.

"What's wrong Lone Wolf," said Little Eagle.

"Thunder woke me and said we had trouble coming, hurry let's go see," said Lone Wolf.

"I hope it isn't serious," said Spirit Wolf.

"Hurry, we will find out, said Little Eagle.

"What is it Thunder," said Lone Wolf.

*"Look off into the distance," said Dark Thunder.*

"What is that," said Spirit Pony.

"It looks like a pack of wolves, how pretty," said Sacred Wolf.

"That's not wolves," said little Eagle.

"No it's not, it's a pack of wild dogs, said Lone Wolf.

*"You are correct, they are more than likely after the horses,"*
*said Dark Thunder.*

"Oh no, what do we do, we don't have time to out run them,"
said Sacred Wolf.

"They are not getting my friends," said Spirit Pony.

"We will think of something," said Lone Wolf.

"Well, you better hurry they are getting closer and we have
no place to hide," said Sacred Wolf.

"Don't panic Sacred Wolf, help us think," said Little Eagle.

"This is the perfect time to panic," said Sacred Wolf.

"What are we going to do Thunder," said Lone Wolf.

*"I cannot tell you. I am only here to warn you of any danger*
*and teach you how to stay on the right path," said Dark Thunder.*

"We best think of something fast, they are getting closer,"
said Sacred Wolf.

"Look, what is making all that dust over there," said Spirit
Wolf.

"Looks like a herd of ponies," said Little Eagle.

"It is, there headed toward the wild dogs," said Lone Wolf.

"Where did they come from," said Sacred Wolf.

"I know where from, right Spirit Pony," said Lone Wolf'.

"How did you know they were here," said Spirit Wolf.

"They are always close by, I sense them, so I ask for their help," said Spirit Pony.

"Look, they are running toward the wild dogs," Little Eagle.

"They ran over the dogs and trampled them," said Lone Wolf.

"One of them got away and is still coming," said Spirit Wolf.

"What are we going to do," said Sacred Wolf.

"Everyone grab a stick or some rocks to throw at it," said Lone Wolf.

"There it is, I am afraid," said Sacred Wolf.

"Girls, get behind Little Eagle and I," said Lone Wolf.

"Throw them rocks at it," said Little Eagle.

"We missed it with the rocks," said Spirit Pony.

"It's getting closer," said Sacred Wolf.

"Look, a wolf came out of nowhere and is stopping the dog from coming any closer," said Lone Wolf.

"The wolf looks really angry," said Spirit Wolf.

"A hawk just hit the dog and knocked it to the ground and now the wolf is all over it," said Lone Wolf.

"Look, the dog is running away with the wolf and the hawk right on its tail," said Little Eagle.

"Yeah, go get it," said Sacred Wolf.

"Have you ever seen anything like that before," said Spirit Pony.

"Where did they come from? We know where the ponies came from, Spirit Pony," said Spirit Wolf.

"That was quick thinking Spirit Pony," said Lone Wolf.

"Yeah Spirit Pony, you saved our lives," said Little Eagle.

"To be honest, I was thinking of the ponies. They are not hurting my ponies, they are my best friend," said Spirit Pony.

"I don't care why you did it, I'm glad you did. I want to give you a thank you hug," said Sacred Wolf.

"A thank you will be suffice, everyone can keep their hugs," said Spirit Pony.

*"I have to say, all of you did a great job. Your parents will be proud when they hear how well you can take care of yourselves," said Dark Thunder.*

"You really think so," said Spirit Wolf.

*"Yes, I know they will, I am," said Dark Thunder.*

"We should eat breakfast, then pack up and head out. We still have a day's journey," said Lone Wolf.

"What are you looking at? Don't even, think about it," said Spirit Pony.

They all looked at Spirit Pony, then at each other. All at once, everyone ran over to Spirit Pony and give her the biggest hug ever. Even though she made out as if she did not like it, you could tell by her slight smile she loved it. As they went to eat, Lone Wolf told the rest to go ahead; he needed to talk to Thunder.

*"What is troubling you Lone Wolf," said Dark Thunder.*

"I don't think anyone else noticed, the wolf and hawk, that was mom and dad wasn't it," said Lone Wolf.

*"They will have to tell you if it was, that is not my place to. I would like to say, you are a wise one and   one day you will be a great Medicine Man," said Dark Thunder.*

"That tells me what I want to know," said Lone Wolf.

*'Don't you tell your parents, let them tell you and you alone? Now, let's go eat,"* said Dark Thunder.

"Don't worry I won't tell anyone," said Lone Wolf.

They joined the rest, ate breakfast, packed the horses, and then prepared to set out on their journey. The day would be long and the stops would only be to water and feed the horses and grabbing a snack for themselves.

They topped a hill and, in the distance, they saw Picketpost Mountian.

"Look everyone, Oak Flats is just a few miles ahead," said Lone Wolf.

"The last one there is a rotten egg," said Little Eagle.

"Hey, that's not fair, you got a head start," said Spirit Pony.

"Don't run them horses to fast, they are tired," said Lone Wolf.

"I'm not racing, I'll stay back with you and Spirit Wolf," said Sacred Wolf.

"I hope the ponies are not too tired, we are not going to be here long are we," said Spirit Wolf.

"No, just long enough to gather samples and see what damage has been done to the water and land," said Lone Wolf.

"That's good. I can't wait to get back home, I feel so dirty," said Sacred Wolf.

"My bracelet feel off my arm, help me find it Spirit Pony," said Little Eagle.

"Okay Little Eagle," said Spirit Pony.

"Look, they are turning around," said Sacred Wolf.

"I wonder why," said Spirit Wolf.

"I don't know, let's go see," said Lone Wolf.

"It fell off somewhere in this area," said Little Eagle.

"We will never find it in among all these rocks, they blend in," said Spirit Pony.

"We have to, Nana will be angry with me if we don't," said Little Eagle.

"No they want, they love us," said Spirit Pony.

"What are you looking for," said Lone Wolf.

 "I lost my bracelet," said Little Eagle.

"Spirit Pony is right, we will never find it." said Sacred Wolf.

"Don't say that." Said Little Eagle.

"They may have a point, the rocks make it blend in," said Spirit Wolf.

"Be quiet everyone, I hear something," said Lone Wolf.

"Sounds like vehicles coming this way," said Little Eagle.

"Spirit Pony, tell the ponies to lay down, said Lone Wolf.

"Okay Lone Wolf," said Spirit Pont.

"Now, lie on their neck and rub them to calm them so they want get up. They will try to when the vehicles pass through," said Lone Wolf.

"I can't believe I am lying on a pony. Now, I smell like a pony," said Sacred Wolf.

"My ponies do not stink," said Spirit Pony.

"Quite everyone, here they come," said Lone Wolf.

"That was a close call," said Little Eagle.

"Hey everyone, I found Little Eagle's bracelet," said Spirit Wolf.

"Think God, we don't have to get any dirtier then I already am," said Sacred Wolf.

"How did you find it," said Little Eagle.

"I happen to see it while I was lying on my pony. It was right in front of my face," said Spirit Wolf.

"Looks like Nana's bracelet's work," said Spirit Pony.

"If that had not happened, they would have seen us," said Lone Wolf.

*"You are right Lone Wolf. Your Nana's was smart to give you protection against danger," said Dark Thunder.*

"I'm glad we found it, but we got to get out of here," said Lone Wolf.

"Lone Wolf is right; we need to get out of here. I fear there may be more headed this way," said Sacred Wolf.

"Are you afraid," said Little Eagle.

"Maybe just a little," said Sacred Wolf.

"Don't let Little Eagle fool you, we all are a little shook up," said Spirit Wolf.

"Not me, this is adventurous," said Little Eagle.

"We don't have time for this. Everyone on your pony, be quite and keep an eye out," said Lone Wolf.

"Be still silly pony," said Sacred Wolf.

"What is wrong," said Spirit Pony.

"This pony will not let me on," said Sacred Wolf.

"Maybe they don't like what you say about them," said Spirit Pony.

"You have got to be kidding me," said Sacred Wolf.

"You know they can understand us," said Spirit Pony.

"Spirit Pony is right, you need to apologize to the ponies," said Little Eagle.

"Okay, I'm sorry. It still will not let me on," said Sacred Wolf.

"You were not sincere with your apology," said Sacred Wolf.

"You are kidding," said Sacred Wolf.

"Come on, we need to get out of this area," said Lone Wolf.

"Okay, Okay. I am sorry for what I said, you are not dirty or silly," said Sacred Wolf.

Everyone starts to snicker.

"That's not funny," said Sacred Wolf.

*"Sacred Wolf is right. Ponies have feelings as we do," said Dark Thunder.*

"We are not laughing cause of that, we are laughing cause we have never seen Sacred Wolf apologize before," said Little Eagle.

*"I did not know, continue," said Dark Thunder.*

"I am sure the pony will let you on now," said Spirit Pony.

"He better, I'm not going to walk. Okay I am on, let's go," said Sacred Spirit.

"You need to hurry Sacred Wolf, we don't have much time," said Lone Wolf.

"I am trying, there is something still wrong with this pony," said Sacred Wolf.

"It may take him a while to forgive you, but he will," said Spirit Pony.

"There, I made it. Ok let's go," said Sacred Wolf.

The pony takes off suddenly, almost causing Sacred Wolf to be thrown from her pony. After a few minutes the rest catch up with her, not long after they arrived at the foot of Oak Flats.

"Did anyone else see all them dead birds and other small animals on the way in," said Lone Wolf.

"I saw them. Why do you think there is so many," said Sacred Wolf.

"The water must be contaminated," said Spirit Wolf.

"We are fixing to find out, there is the creek that runs from the mountain," said Spirit Pony.

"We need to stop here and walk the rest of the way in," said Lone Wolf.

"Why are we walking the rest of the way," said Little Eagle.

"Yeah, I don't fill like walking," said Sacred Wolf.

"We can't take a chance that the horses will try to drink the water," said Lone Wolf.

"We cannot let that happen," said Spirit Pony.

"We are not going to, I will stay with them to make sure, "said Spirt Wolf.

"I will stay with you. I don't want to be anywhere around that dirty water," said Sacred Wolf.

"Okay, the rest of us will go get samples," said Lone Wolf.

"Shew, what is that smell," said Sacred Wolf.

"Look over there, it's a dead horse," said Little Eagle.

"No, I can't believe one of my friends is gone from drinking contaminated water," said Spirit Pony.

*"All animals are our friends," said Dark Thunder.*

"I know, but I have a special bond with the ponies," said Spirit Pony.

*"I understand," said Dark Thunder.*

"We need to go. Water the ponies while we are gone to keep them calm," said Lone Wolf.

"Okay, but hurry the smell unbearable," said Sacred Wolf.

"Have respect for the dead, especially the animals, they do not pollute mother earth," said Little Eagle.

"Your right and I'm sorry, but please hurry," said Sacred Wolf.

"You might as well forget it, Sacred Wolf is who she is," said Spirit Wolf.

"You're telling me," said Little Eagle.

"We are not getting anything done standing around talking," said Sacred Wolf.

"She's right, let's go, we need to hurry," said Lone Wolf.

"I have a bag full of zip lock bags," said Little Eagle.

"Okay, let's go everyone and try to be quite," said Lone Wolf.

"Pick up some of these birds and other small animals on the way to the creek," said Spirit Pony.

"Good idea," said Little Eagle.

"I see all kinds of dead animals," said Spirit Pony.

"I know, it's sad isn't it," said Little Eagle.

"Shew, we are at the creek," said Lone Wolf.

"Look at the water, it has a red color to it," said Spirit Pony.

"That is iron plus other chemicals in the water," said Lone Wolf.

"No wonder there are so many dead animals," said Little Eagle.

*"This is the only creek for a great distance," said Dark Thunder.*

"Give me two sample jars, I want to make sure we have enough for testing," said Lone Wolf.

"I brought a camera, just in case," said Spirit Pony.

"That was smart," said Little Eagle.

"Let me get some picture of the water and the dead animals," said Spirit Pony.

"Here, take a picture of me holding the water with the mountain in the back ground, so everyone will know we were here," said Lone Wolf.

*"Danger is headed this way," said Dark Thunder.*

"Hurry, let's get out of here," said Lone Wolf.

"To late, they are here," said Little Eagle.

"What are you kids doing here," said the mineworker.

"We have enough samples, let's get out of here," said Lone Wolf.

"I am way ahead of you," said Spirit Pony.

"Me to," said Little Eagle,

"You kids stop. What are you doing here," said the mineworker.

The three children make a dash for it, not wanting the workers to find out that they have samples.

★★★★★

"I wish they would hurry," said Sacred Wolf.

"Look, here they come now," said Spirit Wolf.

"Why are they running," said Sacred Wolf.

"I don't know, I'm sure we will find out soon enough," said Spirit Wolf.

"Hurry, get on your ponies, we have to get out of here," said Lone Wolf.

"What's going on," said Sacred Wolf.

"We will tell you later, we got to get away from here," said Spirit Pony.

"You don't have to tell me twice," said Sacred Wolf.

"We just did," said Little Eagle.

"Let's go everybody," said Lone Wolf.

Everyone was so afraid of being caught, they road for almost an hour before slowing.

"I think we can slow down, we left them a ways back," said Lone Wolf.

"That was exciting," said Little Eagle.

"I don't think so, I wasn't even there and I'm still scared," said Sacred Wolf.

"I agree with Sacred Wolf," said Spirit Pony.

"Am I the only one that thinks this is fun," said Little Eagle.

"What do you think Lone Wolf," said Little Eagle.

"I have to think about everyone's safety first. It was sort of fun also," said Lone Wolf.

*"We are not out of danger," said Dark Thunder.*

"Why do you say that," said Sacred Wolf.

*"They have what we call iron horses, I believe you call automobiles," said Dark Thunder.*

"What are you trying to say," said Lone Wolf.

*"They will follow us, they had to go down the creek a ways to cross," said Dark Thunder.*

"That's just great, now what are we going to do," said Sacred Wolf.

"Don't panic, I'm sure we will think of something, right Thunder," said Spirit Pony.

*"We need to make it back to where we camped last night," said Dark Thunder.*

"That's over a half days ride," said Lone Wolf.

*"We will have to ride hard to make it by dark,"* said Dark Thunder.

They rode hard to get back to the campsite before nightfall. The same place they stayed the night before, only stopping long enough to water the ponies. Just as the sun started to set they made it to the final area.

"There's our camp site ahead," said Lone Wolf.

"I can't wait to eat," said Little Eagle.

Minutes later, they arrive at the campsite.

"I thought we would never get here. I am so tired and I feel so dirty," said Sacred Wolf.

"Everyone take the ponies, water and feed them while I fix a fire and something to eat," said Lone Wolf.

*"The miners may be looking for you. I would not build a campfire. You also need to find a place to hide the ponies out of site,"* said Dark Thunder.

"I never thought of that, it's a good idea, thanks Thunder," said Lone Wolf.

*"That's the reason I am here,"* said Dark Thunder.

"We are not going to make a fire. What about all the bugs, not counting the night creatures," said Sacred Wolf.

"What is more important here, keeping creatures away or our lives, "said Spirit Pony.

"I agree with Spirit Pony," said Spirit Wolf.

"All I know is, I am hungry," said Little Eagle.

"Here is the food. Little Eagle and I will hide and feed the ponies, while the rest of you prepare dinner," said Lone Wolf.

"We can do that," said Spirit Pony.

"Let's go find a place to bed down the ponies," said Lone Wolf.

"Okay, I can't wait to eat," said Little Eagle.

"Let's unpack the food, see what we have," said Spirit Wolf.

"I can't believe everyone's so worried about eating, with all the creatures running lose," said Sacred Wolf.

"We have to eat, to keep our strength up for the ride tomorrow," said Spirit Pony.

"I still think we should build a fire, no one is following us," said Sacred Wolf.

"We can't take that chance, if Thunder say's they are following us, then he knows," said Spirit Wolf.

"What if they didn't follow us," said Sacred Wolf.

"That would be even better. We need to concentrate on getting dinner prepared before it gets dark," said Spirit Pony.

*****

"This looks like a good spot to hide the ponies, what do you think Little Eagle," said Lone Wolf.

"It looks perfect," said Little Eagle.

"Let's get the ponies unpacked and feed them, and then we will go eat," said Lone Wolf.

"That sounds good to me, I am starving," said Little Eagle.

"That's what I love about you Little Eagle, you never worry about anything but food," said Lone Wolf.

"I am a growing boy," said Little Eagle.

"Looks like the ponies are almost out of food. They have enough water for one more stop after breakfast tomorrow," said Lone Wolf.

"It's a good thing we are almost home. I miss mom and dad when we are gone for days," said Little Eagle.

"Just remember sometimes they are with us without us knowing," said Lone Wolf.

"Why do you say that, you know something don't you Lone Wolf," said Little Eagle.

"I promised not to tell anyone, but I can trust you. You have to promise you won't tell anyone," said Lone Wolf.

"I promise, you know I won't tell a soul," said Little Eagle.

"Remember yesterday morning when the hawk and wolf attacked that wild dog," said Lone Wolf.

"Yeah, was that mom and dad. I knew it," said Little Eagle.

"You can't say anything to anyone especially them. I gave my word to Thunder, I would not tell anyone. You have to promise you want say a word about it," said Lone Wolf.

"You know I want say anything, we are brothers' I keep my word," said Little Eagle.

"Okay, let's go eat," said Lone Wolf.


✶✶✶✶✶

"Dinner is almost ready, the boy's need to come on," said Spirit Wolf.

"Yeah, I am getting hungry," said Sacred Wolf.

"Here they come now," said Spirit Pony.

"Hey everyone, is dinner ready," said Lone Wolf.

"Yeah, we are starving," said Little Eagle.

"You are always starving," said Spirit Wolf.

"Well, I," said Little Eagle.

"Am a growing boy, we know," said everyone.

"I am," said Little Eagle

After everyone finished dinner they set around and talked about what happened earlier that day and how they could not wait to get home, especially Sacred Wolf. Then they bedded down for the night.

*****

Just before sunrise Lone Wolf was awaken by Dark Thunder.

*"Lone Wolf, Lone Wolf, wake up," said Dark Thunder.*

"What is it Thunder," said Lone Wolf.

*"Come, I need to show you something," said Dark Thunder.*

"Okay, let's go," said Lone Wolf.

"Where are you guys going," said Little Eagle.

*"You come to Little Eagle, but keep quite and keep your head down," said Dark Thunder.*

"Where are we going," said Little Eagle.

*"Shhh, look over there," said Dark Thunder.*

"Is that the miners," said Lone Wolf.

*"Yes," said Dark Thunder.*

"They did follow us," said Little Eagle.

"What is everyone looking at," said Sacred Wolf.

"What are you doing here," said Little Eagle.

"I couldn't sleep, so I followed you," said Sacred Wolf.

*"Be quite, before someone hears you," said Dark Thunder.*

"Is that the miners," said Sacred Wolf.

*"I said, be quiet," said Dark Thunder.*

They grabbed Sacred Wolf by the arm and they laid on the ground watching the miners as they got closer.

*"Get down everyone, keep quiet and don't look at the light, they will be able to see your eyes shining," said Dark Thunder.*

✶✶✶✶✶

The foreman Dan and the lead of operations Brad for the mine was determined to make sure the premises were secure since they saw the young children in the area earlier.

"Shine the spot light on that hill over there, I thought I heard something," said Brad the lead miner.

"I don't see anything," said Dan, miner foreman.

"Did you here that shine the light on the bottom of the hill," said Brad.

"What is that,' said Dan.

"Looks like a pack of wolves," said Brad.

"Let me shoot one of them," said Dan.

"No, if they hear it, we will never find them, let's turn around and go back, we must have past them up," said Dan.

"You don't want to go check out the hill," said Brad.

"No, if they are there the wolves will take care of them for us," said Dan.

"I never thought of that, let's go back, they couldn't have come this far," said Brad.


*****


"What, he better not shoot one of my wolves," said Sacred Wolf.

"Be quiet and get down, you are going to get us caught," said Little Eagle.

*"You can get up now, they are gone," said Dark Thunder.*

"Was that the miners," said Spirit Wolf.

"Where did you two come from," said Lone Wolf.

"We got here about a minute before they left, we heard Sacred Wolf," said Spirit Pony.

"They were going to shoot the wolves," said Sacred Wolf.

"What wolves," said Spirit Wolf.

"There is a pack at the bottom of the hill," said Sacred Wolf.

"Where, we want to see them," said Spirit Wolf.

*"This was to be Lone Wolf and I alone," said Dark Thunder.*

"We always work together as a team," said Little Eagle.

*"That is what I wanted to hear. Always stand together as one," said Dark Thunder.*

"They are gone, what do we do now," said Spirit Pony.

"I say we feed and water the ponies, eat a bite, then leave as soon as possible, before they return," said Lone Wolf.

*"That is a wise move," said Dark Thunder.*

"Little Eagle and I will feed the ponies while the rest of you fix something to eat," said Lone Wolf.

"I wish I had a place to take a bath. I fill so dirty I can hardly stand myself," said Sacred Wolf.

"We could all use a bath," said Spirit Wolf.

"Let's go Little Eagle, so we can eat and get out of here," said Lone Wolf.

"That's the best news I have heard all morning. I'm right behind you," said Little Eagle.

"Let's get something ready to eat so we can head home," said Spirit Pony.

"I can't wait to get home," said Sacred Wolf.

"We are almost out of food and water for the ponies," said Little Eagle.

"I noticed the same thing. We will give them all the feed left and save enough water for one more stop," said Lone Wolf.

I can't wait to get home to get some good food," said Little Eagle.

"I don't want to sound like Sacred Wolf, but I can't wait to take a shower," said Lone Wolf.

"You do sound a little like Sacred Wolf," said Little Eagle.

"Whatever you do, don't let her know I said that," said Lone Wolf.

"You don't have to worry, I won't," said Little Eagle.

"Now that we have feed the ponies let's get them ready for the ride home," said Lone Wolf.

"I can't wait to get home, now I am starting to sound like Sacred Wolf," said Little Wolf.

"Breakfast is ready, said Spirit Wolf.

"I wonder where the guys are," said Sacred Wolf.

"There they are," said Spirit Pony.

"Breakfast is ready," said Spirit Wolf.

"Yeah, if we hurry we can make it back home soon," said Sacred Wolf.

"If we leave in the next thirty minutes we should make it home by three or so," said Lone Wolf'

*"Lone Wolf is right; there is a good chance the miners may come back. They will stop at nothing to get this mine under way," said Dark Thunder.*

"In that case, I am ready to go now," said Sacred Wolf.

"We have to eat first," said Little Eagle.

"What is more important, our stomachs or our lives," said Sacred Wolf.

"Little Eagle is right, we have to eat first," said Spirit Pony.

"I agree,' said Spirit Wolf.

"I think we all agree, you need to calm down and we will be leaving soon," said Lone Wolf.

"Okay, I will try," said Sacred Wolf.

They finished breakfast then headed home, only to stop once to water the horses. The ride home would be a long one, but hopefully they would get home by dark but all  depends on how fast they rode. No one spoke much on the way back; no one could wait to get home. Just before dark they arrived home. They stopped upon a hill where they could see their home in the distance.

"Look over there, that's where the house is. We are only twenty minutes away," said Lone Wolf.

"I am so hungry, I can't wait," said Little Eagle.

"Neither can I. The last one there has to take a shower last," said Sacred Wolf.

"Hold up Sacred Wolf, we can't run the ponies, they are tired and hungry," said Lone Wolf.

"I can't wait to take a shower, I don't know who smells the worse me or this pony," said Sacred Wolf.

At that time, the pony reared up and Sacred Wolf fell off.

"Now you have a reason to take a shower," said Spirit Wolf.

"Look at all the dirt on my cloths," said Sacred Wolf.

"That's nothing, you should see your face and hair," said Little Eagle.

"There is dirt in my hair. That stupid pony," said Sacred Wolf.

"I told you, you cannot say mean things about the ponies, they can understand you,' said Spirit Pony.

"That silly pony better let me back on. I will not walk all the way home," said Sacred Wolf.

"Don't count on it. Spirit Pony told you and you called him a name again," said Lone Wolf.

"It better let me on. Stop moving pony," said Sacred Wolf.

"You will have to apology and be serious, they know if you are or not," said Spirit Pony.

"You can't be serious, I apologized once already," said Sacred Wolf.

"You didn't keep your word. You called him a bad name again, when you promised you wouldn't again," said Spirit Pony.

"Okay, I get it, always keep your word no matter what," said Sacred Wolf.

*"If you do keep your word, every living thing will learn to trust you," said Dark Thunder.*

"I see. I am sorry pony, I will never call you a bad name again," said Sacred Wolf.

"I thought I have seen everything," said Little Eagle.

"Look everyone I am on my pony and I think we will get along this time," said Sacred Wolf.

*"This is where we part ways," said Dark Thunder.*

"Will we see you again," said Spirit Wolf.

*"You will see me again, especially on your next journey," said Dark Thunder.*

"I want to thank you, I don't know what may have happened if you had not been there," said Lone Wolf.

*"It was my honor to walk with all of you, especially the one that hates getting dirty," said Dark Thunder.*

"Bye Thunder, bye," said everyone.

"Getty up pony," said Sacred Wolf.

"What is your big hurry Sacred Wolf," said Little Eagle.

"To take a shower, where do you think I'm going," said Sacred Wolf.

"For you and her to look alike, you are nothing alike,' said Spirit Pony.

"I am glad for that, I would drive myself crazy,' said Spirit Wolf.

"Look at her go. Have you ever seen anyone want to take a shower so bad," said Spirit Pony.

"I can't say I blame her, but its food I want," said Little Eagle.

"If it wasn't for taking care of the ponies first, I would say go ahead," said Lone Wolf.

"I know," said Little Eagle.

"Spirit Wolf and I can help you, if Little Eagle wants to go ahead. If that's okay with Spirit Wolf," said Spirit Pony.

"That's fine with me," said Spirit Wolf.

"Thanks you guys, Getty up pony," said Little Eagle.

"I can't believe you two did that," said Lone Wolf.

"He must be starving, did you hear how pitiful he sounded," said Spirit Wolf.

$$\star\star\star\star\star$$

"Hi Sacred Wolf, you back, " said Spirit Hawk.

"I don't have time mom, I need a shower," said Sacred Wolf.

"Sounds like she needs a shower really bad," said Little Wolf.

"Can you imagine her going this long without a shower, she must be beside her self," said Spirit Hawk.

"Did you see the dirt in her hair," said Little Wolf.

"It was all over her face too," said Spirit Hawk.

"The rest of them must have had a blast teasing her about it, said Little Wolf.

"That would be funny, I'm the same way," said Spirit Hawk.

"Yes, I know, but you know how children are, especially around Sacred Wolf. I love the way she is, but children will be children," said Little Wolf.

"Is that because she is so much like her mother, I love you to," said Spirit Hawk.

"Hi mom, dad," said Little Eagle.

"How was your trip son," said Little Wolf.

"Don't have time dad, I'm starving," said Little Eagle.

"What is up with these kids," said Little Wolf.

"Sounds like they are dirty and hungry," said Spirit Hawk.

"I can't wait to see what's wrong with the rest of them," said Little Wolf.

"I'm sure they all will be hungry and need a shower," said Spirit Wolf.

"You want to go out on the porch to see where the others are," said Little Wolf.

"I would love to, I can't wait to see them all," said Spirit Hawk.


* * * * *


As they stepped outside, the sun was setting. The night sky was so mystical.

"They left the gear on the ponies," said Little Wolf.

"The ponies look tired and thirsty," said Spirit Hawk.

"You want to go with me to take them to the water trough. Look, here comes the other kids now," said Little Wolf.

"You go ahead, I'm going to go into the kitchen where Little Eagle is and start dinner," said Spirit Hawk.

"Okay, I will tend to these horses. We will be in as soon as possible," said Little Wolf.


* * * * *


"Hi Little Eagle, don't eat too much, dinner will be ready shortly," said Spirit Hawk.

"Don't worry mom, I can eat no matter how full I am," said Little Eagle.

"That is a sign of a true apache, they have always been able to put the food away," said Spirit Hawk.

"Moo, moo, moo," said Little Eagle.

"Don't talk with a mouth full son," said Spirit Hawk.

"Okay mom," said Little Eagle.

"What am I going to do with that boy," said Spirit Hawk.

*****

"Hey dad, what are you doing," said Lone Wolf.

"Taking these ponies to the water trough, go ahead and bring the others over here," said Little Wolf.

"Did you see Sacred Wolf and Little Eagle," said Lone Wolf.

"Yes, I sure did, one was wanting a shower while the other was eating" said Little Wolf.

"Little Eagle sounded like he was starving to death," said Spirit Wolf.

"Yeah and Sacred Wolf sounded like she was never going to stop complaining over a shower," said Spirit Pony.

"Well, your sister hates dirt. She takes that after her mother," said Little Wolf.

"Yeah we know dad. We love her and all, but our ears sometimes hurt having to listen to it," said Spirit Pony.

"I have to agree with her dad and I'm her identical twin," said Spirit Wolf.

"Why don't you kids go on in the house? Dinner will be ready shortly. I will water the ponies," said Little Wolf.

"Are you serious, let's go Spirit Pony," said Spirit Wolf.

"You girls go ahead, I'm going to help dad," said Lone Wolf.

"Okay," said Spirit Pony.

"You look tired son, why don't you go in and get ready for dinner," said Little Wolf.

"Dad, you know I can sense what wrong when you are troubled," said Lone Wolf.

"I sometimes forget about you being able to do that. It's nothing though son, go on in," said Little Wolf.

"I'm not going to leave until you do, so please tell me," said Lone Wolf.

"You are head strong, just like your mother," said Little Wolf.

"I know, so tell me what's wrong," said Lone Wolf.

"Well son I don't know if you have noticed or not, you sister Sacred Wolf is more like your mother then any of you, not saying that the rest of you aren't a lot like her, you are," said Little Wolf.

"Yeah dad I know. All of us are you and mom all rolled up into one," said Lone Wolf.

"Well said son," said Little Wolf.

"Go ahead dad, don't try to change the subject," said Lone Wolf.

"You are like your mother. How do I say this? Sacred Wolf is so much like your mom, if something was to happen to your mother she the closes one I have to remind me of her," said Little Wolf.

"Dad, nothing is going to happen to either one of you, so don't talk like that. Both of you are going to live to be a hundred years old," said Lone Wolf.

"I don't know about that son. I would like your mom and I to be on this world long enough to see all the kids make something of their lives, cause you are the smartest kids I ever meet," said Little Wolf.

"That's because we take after mom," said Lone Wolf.

"I don't disagree with that. I want you to know I love your mother with all my heart," said Little Wolf.

"I know dad. Can I ask you something and be honest," said Lone Wolf.

"Sure son, I wouldn't have it any other way," said Little Wolf.

"Is mom okay," said Lone Wolf.

"Yes son she's fine," said Little Wolf.

"Then why are you so worried for dad," said Lone Wolf.

"Your mother has been worried about all of you when you go on these journey's, it got me to thinking about what I would do if something happened to her," said Little Wolf.

"Dad, we had Thunder with us," said Lone Wolf.

"I know son, you couldn't ask for a better guide to watch over you. Thunder is a spirit, he cannot interfere, he is there to warn you of any danger, you have to figure out how to get out of it yourself," said Little Wolf.

"I understand dad, we will be careful when we are on a journey," said Lone Wolf.

"Your mom and I would fill better if you do," said Little Wolf.

"By the way dad, I know it was you and mom who ran the wolves off," said Lone Wolf.

"Did Thunder tell you," said Little Wolf.

"No, I figured it out myself," said Lone Wolf.

"You are a wise one son. Let's go eat," said Little Wolf.

"Okay, I love you dad," said Lone Wolf.

"I love you to son," said Little Wolf.

"I almost forgot, here are the samples we gathered at Oak Flats," said Lone Wolf.

"I will take them to the lab first thing tomorrow," said Little Wolf.

"You should have seen what the mining company is doing to the land and animals," said Lone Wolf.

"The mining companies don't care about the land or animals. They only want what's in the ground and they don't care about the devastation left behind," said Little Wolf.

"There were dead animals everywhere," said Lone Wolf.

"That's what happens when mines are allowed to come in and take over. The land can be destroyed for miles and the water can be contaminated for hundreds of miles," said Little Wolf.

"There is nothing in the ground worth the land being destroyed that way," said Lone Wolf.

"I agree with you son. Mother Earth should be treated as a paradise and left the way the Creator intended it to be," said Little Wolf.

"It's sad so many people suffer for so few to get rich," said Lone Wolf.

"Would you like to ride with me to the lab tomorrow," said Little Wolf.

"I would like that dad," said Lone Wolf.

"We better go in, you need to get ready for dinner before your mother starts worrying about us," said Little Wolf.

"It's a little late for that dad. Mom worries all the time about everything," said Lone Wolf.

"That's because she loves you so much," said Little Wolf.

"I know. I will race you to the house," said Lone Wolf.

"Hey, you got a head start," said Little Wolf.

"I won," said Lone Wolf.

'Yes you did son," said Little Wolf.

"I think you let me win dad," said Lone Wolf.

"I had no choice, you were half way there when I started," said Little Wolf.

Lone Wolf and his dad laughed as they entered the house. They had never felt so close before. The children were becoming grownups, and will one day, find their own path to follow. The next day Lone Wolf, Little Eagle, and dad took the samples to the lab to be tested. A week later the samples showed high levels of copper, lead, and mercury. All three considered highly toxic if not handled proper. Two weeks later the mining stopped, for how long no one knows. We hope forever. The kids were happy to know they can make a difference.

Three weeks passed since the children visited Oak Flats. They hope to one-day return to look around without being ran off by miners. The family were setting around talking about Oak Flats, when something about Apache Leap was mentioned.

"You look nice mom," said Spirit Wolf.

"Your mom is beautiful no matter what she wears," said Little Wolf.

"What is that pretty neckless you have on," said Sacred Wolf.

"I have never seen a stone like it before," said Spirit Pony.

"It is beautiful, what kind of stone is it mom," said Spirit Wolf.

"Your dad gave it to me," said Spirit Hawk.

"Where did you find it dad," said Lone Wolf.

"I found it at a place called Apache Leap," said Little Wolf.

"Apache Leap, where is it and how did the stones get there," said Little Eagle.

"That is a long and tragic story," said Little Wolf.

"I love stories," said Little Eagle.

"I want to hear about Apache Leap myself," said Lone Wolf.

"It's sad, what happen many years ago at Apache Leap," said Little Wolf.

"What's that dad," said Spirit Pony.

"Your dads talking about the tragic that took place many years ago," said Spirit Hawk.

"What happen that was so tragic," said Spirit Wolf.

"We never got around to telling you children about Apache Leap and the Apache Tears," said Little Wolf.

"What are Apache Tears," said Little Eagle.

"I can't wait to hear this story," said Lone Wolf.

"It all started when a band of Apaches found a secret passage to the top of one of the mountains at Oak Flats," said Little Wolf.

"That's where we took our last adventure trip," said Lone Wolf.

"Yes it was, son. When the band of Apaches made it to the top, they knew it would the safest place for them to be. They could see anyone approach from all four sides of the mountain. Their families would also be safe while they were on a hunting trip," said Little Wolf.

"This story sounds exciting already," said Little Eagle.

"Shhh, I want to hear the story," said Spirit Pony.

"For years they lived on the mountain in peace. One day the Calvary came through and with what is known as a spy class use to see objects up close, they saw movement on the mountain," said Little Wolf.

"Why didn't they hide," said Sacred Wolf.

"The Calvary was so far away they didn't know, remember they had a spy class," said Little Wolf.

"Oh yeah," said Sacred Wolf.

"What happened dad," said Lone Wolf?

"One morning before daylight the Calvary found the hidden trail and took all their men to the top of the mountain and surprised the Apaches," said Little Wolf.

"Didn't they have look outs to let them know, Thunder taught us that," said Little Eagle.

"Yes they did son, but the lookout had fallen asleep. The Calvary intended on taking the Apaches as prisoners. Some were shot attempting to overtake the Calvary. The warriors realized they had nowhere to go and they would not surrender to the Calvary. So, they made their way to the edge of the cliff, warriors never surrender. The rest of the Apache Warriors seeing they were out gunned took it on themselves to die a warriors death, to throw themselves off the mountain," said Little Wolf.

"Why didn't they surrender and escape later," said Spirit Pony.

"They knew if taken prisoner, they would be tortured and killed. That would have been a disgrace as a warrior. So, they chose to throw themselves off the cliffs," said Lone Wolf.

"That is correct son," said Little Wolf.

"That is a true warriors death," said Lone Wolf.

"That's so said," said Spirit Wolf.

"Yes, it is son, so then when the women and children saw their men on the cliffs dead, they whelped. The tears fell to the sand and the Creator formed them into what we call Apache Tears," said Little Wolf.

"That is a sad story," said Spirit Wolf.

"Yes it is, that's why we have these Apache Tears to remind us of what happen back then," said Spirit Hawk.

"There has to be more to the story of Apache Tears then that," said Spirit Pony.

"Good observation Spirit Pony," said Little Wolf.

"I knew there was more to the Apache Tear," said Spirit Pony.

"They are known to make you think positive and keep evil away," said Little Wolf.

"We could use a bunch of them," said Little Eagle.

"We sure could, with all the danger we run into," said Sacred Wolf.

"Have you run into more danger," said Little Wolf.

"Nothing we can't handle," said Lone Wolf.

"As you all know your mother worries about you. You must always put safety first," said Little Wolf.

"Are you not afraid dad," said Little Eagle.

"Of course I am. I trust your judgement and I trust Thunder to keep you protected and safe," said Little Wolf.

"I can't wait to go see Apache Leap," said Lone Wolf.

"Me to, I want to make some jewelry using Apache Tears," said Spirit Wolf.

"That would be pretty," said Spirit Pony.

"We don't have time this week end," said Lone Wolf.

"Your mom and I know a way, you can go and return in one day," said Little Wolf.

"How is that dad, fly like I do," said Little Eagle.

"Forget it, I'm not flying, I like my feet on the ground," said Sacred Wolf.

"Flying is neat, once you get the hang of it," said Little Eagle.

"No, I'm not going to fly. How are we going to take supplies," said Sacred Wolf.

"If everyone will calm down I will tell you," said Little Wolf.

"They always over react before knowing everything," said Lone Wolf.

"How can we get there and back in one day dad," said Spirit Pony.

"Your mom and I was going to wait for the right time to tell you, we think you are ready now," said Little Wolf.

"Tell us dad, I can't wait to hear," said Sacred Wolf.

"See what I mean dad, they have no patience's," said Lone Wolf.

"Lone Wolf is right. Patience is a virtue," said Little Wolf

"Dad, come on," said Sacred Wolf.

"Okay, have any of you ever heard of a portal hole," said Spirit Hawk.

"I have, it's a way to travel great distances in a matter of minutes," said Spirit Pony.

"You are somewhat right. It could take a few hours to travel a great distance," said Spirit Hawk.

"That sounds cool, how do we open a portal hole," said Little Eagle.

"It will take all of you, but as you get older you will be able to do it on your own," said Little Wolf.

"What do we do to open the portal hole?" said Spirit Wolf.

"To start with, you will need a potion jar and a candle," said Spirit Hawk.

"I know where a candle is, but where are we going to get a potion jar," said Spirit Pony.

"I have one you can us," said Spirit Hawk.

"What are you doing with a potion jar mom," said Spirit Wolf.

"I use it for certain things," said Spirit Hawk.

"Are you a witch mom," said Sacred Wolf.

"I am a good witch," said Spirit Hawk.

"Is there different kinds of witches," said Little Eagle.

"You have good witches and bad witches. A good witch only does good things a bad witch does only mean things," said Spirit Hawk.

"Can you teach us mom," said Spirit Pony.

"I sure can, just let me know when you want to start," said Spirit Hawk.

"We can start right now," said Sacred Wolf.

"Has everyone forgotten we are going to Apache Leap tomorrow? We need to learn how to open a portal hole," said Lone Wolf.

"Lone Wolf is right, I can show you girls another day about witchcraft," said Spirit Hawk.

"Okay we can't wait. We really want to learn more about witchcraft," said Spirit Pony.

"Good, we don't have time for that," said Little Eagle.

"Do you have time to learn to be a warlock," said Little Wolf.

"A warlock, are you serious dad. Are you a warlock," said Little Eagle.

"Yes I am son and all of you are good witches and warlocks, we do only good things," said Little Wolf.

"When can you teach us dad," said Little Eagle.

"I thought there wasn't time for that," said Spirit Wolf.

"This is different, we are warlocks," said Little Eagle.

"That's how it is, it's not important unless it's about you guys," said Sacred Wolf.

**80**

"That's not what I meant, it's just," said Little Eagle.

"We know what you meant," said Spirit Pony.

"Listen up everyone," said Little Wolf.

"But dad," said Spirit Pony,

"Give me a minute, I'm sure your brother didn't mean anything by that did you son," said Little Wolf.

"But dad," said Little Eagle.

"Okay son apologize to your sisters, now," said Little Wolf.

"Okay, I'm sorry," said Little Eagle.

"You see son, witches and warlock are the same, the only difference is witches are women and warlocks are men," said Little Wolf.

"I hate to interrupt everyone, but can we get back to the Apache Tears and learning how to teleport, I want to learn about being a warlock to, but first things first. This is about Apache Tears. We can concentrate on that some other time," said Lone Wolf.

"Lone Wolf is right. When you do a task always do one at a time, or you may lose your concentration, then someone could get hurt," said Spirit Hawk.

"Your right mom, we will learn about witchcraft some other time," said Spirit wolf.

"Yeah, we can learn about warlocks too dad later. By the way girls, I'm sorry for what I said earlier," said Little Eagle.

"Now I have everyone's attention, how do you teleport," said Lone Wolf.

"I'm going to let your mom handle this one. It's more her cup of tea," said Little Wolf.

"First you need to form a circle and hold hands. Now close your eyes and see in your mind what the place looks like, if you have never seen the place you want to go, then repeat the name of the place over and over and don't forget to concentrate," said Spirit Hawk.

"Okay everyone close your eyes and think Apache Leap," said Lone Wolf.

As the children closed their eyes and concentrated on the area, they portal started to open. The bright lights surround them and it was breathtaking.

"Its opening kids, keep concentrating," said Spirit Hawk.

"It disappeared," said Little Wolf.

"What happen to it," said Lone Wolf?

"I think someone lost concentration," said Spirit Hawk.

"Wonder who that was, Sacred Wolf," said Lone Wolf.

"Don't be so rough on her, she will need to practice more," said Little Wolf.

"Sorry my mind was on something else. Let's try it again," said Sacred Wolf.

"Okay everyone, let's try it again and this time concentrate," said Lone Wolf.

"It's working, hold your concentration for a few more seconds," said Spirit Hawk.

"You did it kid's, open your eyes and look," said Little Wolf.

"Wow, that is beautiful," said Spirit Pony.

"Isn't it," said Spirit Wolf.

"So, that's what Apache Leap looks like," said Lone Wolf.

"I'm ready to go now," said Little Eagle.

"You have time, long as you are home by dinner," said Little Wolf.

"Who wants to go," said Lone Wolf.

"Not me, I don't want to play in the dirt," said Sacred Wolf.

"I thought you wanted some Apache Tears," said Little Eagle.

"I do, I was hoping you guys could bring me some," said Sacred Wolf.

"You're kidding, right," said Little Wolf.

"I will try to find you some," said Spirit Pony.

"Think you Spirit Pony, I owe you one," said Sacred Wolf.

"Let's go, I can't wait," said Lone Wolf.

"Hold up, after everyone goes through, the last person needs to close the portal hole," said Spirit Hawk.

"How do we do that," said Lone Wolf.

"The last one through needs to say close porthole," said Spirit Hawk.

"I'm going to grab some water," said Spirit Pony.

"Good ideal, I'll help you," said Spirit Wolf.

"More delays," said Little Eagle.

"The girls are right, we need water," said Lone Wolf.

"Yeah I know, it's just, why couldn't I have thought of it," said Little Eagle.

Lone Wolf pushes him on the shoulder and says.

"Silly, they can think of things to," said Lone Wolf.

"Lone Wolf is right, you boys job is to protect them not to think for them," said Little Wolf.

"Your right dad, I never thought of like that. Hurry up girls," said Little Eagle.

"We are coming, don't rush us," said Spirit Pony.

"Yeah, we did think of water, we will need it," said Spirit Wolf.

Little Eagle looks at Lone Wolf with a smirk on his face and pushes him and says.

"You girls did well, I am glad you thought of water," said Lone Wolf.

"Yeah, quick thinking," said Little Eagle.

"Everyone ready," said Lone Wolf.

"You sure you don't want to go Sacred Wolf," said Spirit Wolf.

"It won't be the same without you there," said Spirit Pony.

"I don't want to dig in the dirt," said Sacred Wolf.

"Little Eagle and I will find them for you," said Lone Wolf.

"You will," said Sacred Wolf.

"We will," said Little Eagle.

"Of course, we will. You are our sister and we love you," said Lone Wolf.

"Yeah, it is more fun when you are there," said Little Eagle.

"Okay, I will go, but I'm not getting dirty," said Sacred Wolf.

"Good, we wanted you to, but didn't want to pressure you," said Spirit Wolf.

"You know it wouldn't be the same without you there," said

Spirit Pony.

"Yeah, who else are we going to get a laugh out of," said Little Eagle.

"He's kidding, come on, let's go," said Lone Wolf.

"See you later, mom and dad," said Sacred Wolf.

"Yeah mom, dad, we will be back soon," said Spirit Pony.

"Around dinner time," said Little Eagle.

"That is all you think about," said Sacred Wolf.

"Sometimes I think about sleep," said Little Eagle.

"Let me guess, you dream about food," said Spirit Pony.

"Sometimes," said Little Eagle.

"Come on everyone, bye mom, dad," said Lone Wolf.

"We love you mom, dad," said Sacred Wolf.

"We love you. Be careful children," said Spirit Hawk.

"We will mom," said Spirit Wolf.

"Don't forget to close the porthole behind you," said Spirit Hawk.

"We will, bye," said Spirit Pony.

"I still worry about them being alone," said Spirit Hawk.

"I know, I worry too. I'm sure Thunder will be there," said Little Wolf.

"I hope so," said Spirit Hawk.

The children pass through the porthole and could not believe the beauty of Apache Leap.

"This place looks awesome," said Lone Wolf.

"It is pure beauty," said Spirit Wolf.

"No wonder the Apaches liked this place," said Sacred Wolf.

"Close porthole," said Spirit Pony.

"Let's climb to the top," said Little Eagle.

"We will, I think we should find Apache Leap first," said Lone Wolf.

"It's this way," said Sacred Wolf.

"How do you know," said Spirit Wolf.

"A feeling I have," said Sacred Wolf.

"Okay everyone, this way," said Lone Wolf.

The children made their way around the foot of Apache Leap.

"Hold up everyone. This is the spot where it happened," said Sacred Wolf.

"You sure," said Spirit Pony.

"Yeah, this is the place," said Sacred Wolf.

"There's one way to make sure. Look for the Apache Tears," said Little Eagle.

"I found one already," said Spirit Wolf.

"We need to dig in the sand," said Lone Wolf.

"I found one, " said Little Eagle.

"I found one too " said Lone Wolf.

"Sacred Wolf, why are you crying," said Spirit Pony.

"I can fill the sadness of the Apache women and children when they saw their warriors bodies," said Sacred Wolf.

"Don't cry, you want to go for a walk." said Spirit Pony.

"No, I'm okay," said Sacred Wolf.

*"You are filling sad, cause you are standing in a spot where one of the warriors wives as you call them, stood and whelped,"* said Dark Thunder.

"Thunder, you're here," said Sacred Wolf.

They all ran and gave Thunder the biggest hug. Of course, Sacred Wolf was the first to reach him.

*"I am always watching over you, all of you. Especially this one,"* said Dark Thunder.

Thunder rubs Sacred Wolf on the head and tells them to go back to looking for Apache Tears.

"We love you Uncle Thunder," said Sacred Wolf.

*"I love all of you too, now let's start looking for Apache Tears, you may be surprised what you will find,"* said Dark Thunder.

"Come on everyone," said Little Eagle.

"I found one," said Lone Wolf.

"Look everybody, I found a handful," said Little Eagle.

"Them wasn't there a few minutes ago," said Spirit Wolf.

"That is where Sacred Wolf was standing when she was crying," said Spirit Pony.

"I found them," said Little Eagle.

*"Spirit Pony is right, those are Sacred Wolves actual tears,"* said Dark Thunder.

"Those are my tears inside them," said Sacred Wolf.

"Yes *they are*," *said Dark Thunder.*

"Here Sacred Wolf, I told you I would find you some Apache Tears. I had no idea they would actually be yours," said Little Eagle.

"Thank you Little Eagle, I love you," said Sacred Wolf.

"You don't have to get so mushy, I love you to," said Little Eagle.

"Let's get back to digging, we still have to climb Apache Leap," said Lone Wolf.

"I can't wait to see what might be on top of Apache Leap," said Little Eagle.

"Neither can I," said Lone Wolf.

"They looked for the Apache Tears until all of them had two handfuls. Then it was time to climb Apache Leap.

"I think we have plenty of Apache Tears," said Lone Wolf.

"Yeah, now let's climb the mountain," said Little Eagle.

"You guys go ahead, it's too dirty," said Sacred Wolf.

"Come with us, it want be the same without you," said Spirit Wolf.

"I don't want to be a burden for anyone," said Sacred Wolf.

"You're not a burden, is she guys," said Spirit Pony.

"I've heard the boys talk like I am," said Sacred Wolf.

"We don't mean it like that," said Lone Wolf.

"Then how do you mean it, Little Eagle," said Sacred Wolf.

"We only say what we do to get a laugh. Without you with us, it would get boring and that's no fun," said Little Eagle.

"So, I'm fun to be around," said Sacred Wolf.

"Well, I wouldn't go that far," said Little Eagle.

"Too late, you already said I was fun. I'll go with you," said Sacred Wolf.

"Oh boy, what have I done," said Little Eagle.

*"What you did was a good thing. Look how happy you made her Little Eagle," said Dark Thunder.*

"Your right, she looks very happy," said Little Eagle.

"If everyone through crying, we need to go," said Lone Wolf.

As Little Eagle wipes a tear off his cheek, he tells Lone Wolf.

"I'm not crying, there is dust in my eyes," said Little Eagle.

"If that's what you want to tell yourself little brother, I understand," said Lone Wolf.

*"Even grown men cry. That shows you have a heart," said Dark Thunder.*

"Yeah, little brother," said Little Eagle.

"Is everyone ready to climb Apache Leap," said Lone Wolf.

"We have plenty of Apache Tears," said Spirit Pony.

"Yeah, I can't wait to see what's on top, " said Little Eagle.

"You guy's better help me, I don't want to get dirty. If I do I will cry," said Sacred Wolf.

"We will help you if you don't cry," said Lone Wolf.

"Yeah, anything but that," said Little Eagle.

"I knew that would get you, okay, I'm ready to go," said Sacred Wolf.

They went to find the path to the top. They knew which side of the mountain to look on. Finding the path would be a different story. Not many people climb to the top, for the path was growned up and not visible. After an hour or so they finally found the way to the top.

"I found it, over here," said Little Eagle.

"It's about time, my feet are starting to hurt just standing here," said Sacred Wolf.

"No wonder it was so hard to find, it's grown up bad," said Lone Wolf.

*"The spirits that watch out for the mountain did this to keep people out," said Dark Thunder.*

"They must be really angry, it's growned up pretty bad," said Spirit Wolf.

"Can you blame them after what happen," said Lone Wolf.

"No, I can't," said Spirit Wolf.

"I can't get through there, I might hang my clothes on a limb and tear them," said Sacred Wolf.

"We will hold the limbs why you pass them, want we Little Eagle," said Lone Wolf.

"I guess," said Little Eagle.

"I don't need any help, I can do it myself," said Spirit Pony.

"Follow me, I'll go first, since I found the path," said Little Eagle.

Everybody go ahead of me. I'll go last," said Lone Wolf.

"I can't get through cause of these limbs," said Sacred Wolf.

"I will hold it back for you," said Little Eagle.

"That's better Little Eagle," said Sacred Wolf.

"Wait on me after everyone gets through," said Little Eagle.

"Okay, ouch," said Sacred Wolf.

"Sorry, the limb slipped out of my hand," said Little Eagle.

"I bet it slipped," said Sacred Wolf.

"What is going on here," said Lone Wolf.

"Little Eagle let a limb go and hit me in my butt," said Sacred Wolf.

They all sniggered to themselves.

"That was not funny, it hurt," said Sacred Wolf.

*"She is right, it isn't funny. Did you do it on purpose," said Dark Thunder.*

"Well, she makes you fill like it is our job to do things for her," said Little Eagle.

*"Did you not say that you would help her if she came along," said Dark Thunder.*

"But I," said Little Eagle.

*"No you agreed if she came along you would help her. You know she didn't want to come, but you said you would help her," said Dark Thunder.*

"He is right. That is what we agreed on," said Spirit Wolf.

"Yeah your right, I'm sorry," said Little Eagle.

"That is okay, I can't help it I'm a girly girl," said Sacred Wolf.

"I wouldn't want you to be any other way," said Little Eagle.

They finally made it to the top of the mountain. It was not as easy as they thought cause the path was grown up with shrubs. They could not believe what they saw when they got to the top. It was almost as if they had stepped back into time.

"We are at the top," said Little Eagle.

"It looks as if they are still living here," said Spirit Pony.

"Not hardly, but it looks like no one has touched anything," said Lone Wolf.

"Look, here are some arrowheads," said Little Eagle.

*"Don't touch anything," said Dark Thunder.*

"Why not," said Spirit Pony.

*"This is a sacred mountain. The spirits that gave their lives on the mountain still watch over it. If you disturb anything, you will anger the spirits," said Dark Thunder.*

"We don't want them angry at us," said Sacred Wolf.

"We got what we came after. Leave everything else alone," said Lone Wolf.

"I am ready to leave," said Sacred Wolf.

"We will leave in a few minutes," said Lone Wolf.

"We have a long walk back down the mountain," said Sacred Wolf.

"We are not walking back down, we will use the porthole to go home from here," said Lone Wolf.

"Wait, we can use the porthole. Why did we climb on foot then," said Sacred Wolf.

"So we could see what our ancestors went through," said Lone Wolf.

"I can't believe we walk up this path and didn't have to," said Sacred Wolf.

"I thought it was cool. Look at it as an adventure," said Spirit Pony.

"It's time to head home," said Lone Wolf.

"I can't wait," said Sacred Wolf.

"Everyone, concentrate on home," said Lone Wolf.

"I see it. It's open," said Sacred Wolf.

"Let's go everyone, I am starving," said Little Eagle.

"I'll take a shower while you eat," said Sacred Wolf.

"I can't wait to see my Apache Tears up close," said Spirit Pony.

"Yeah, and see what kind of jewelry I can make out of them," said Spirit Wolf.

"Let's go everyone, worry about all that after we get home," said Lone Wolf.

"You coming Thunder," said Sacred Wolf.

"When will we see you again," said Spirit Wolf.

They all ran to him, hugged him and told him how much they loved him.

*"I will see you on your next journey," said Dark Thunder.*

"Bye Thunder," said the children.

*"Bye children," said Dark Thunder.*

"Close Porthole," said Spirit Pony.

Spirit Hawk and Little Wolf were standing on the porch when the children returned.

"Look there come's the children," said Spirit Hawk.

"Hi mom, dad, wait till you see all the Apache Tears we found," said Spirit Wolf.

"It was something else," said Lone Wolf.

"It was fun," said Little Eagle.

"If you call getting dirty fun," said Sacred Wolf.

"Look at all the Apache Tears we found. Sacred Wolf cried and her tears turned into the stone," said Spirit Pony.

"She did, can I see them," said Spirit Hawk.

"Here mom, you hang on to them while I take a shower," said Sacred Wolf.

"Dad, have you ever been on top of Apache Leap," said Little Eagle.

"Not in many years," said Little Wolf.

"Here dad, you can look at mine while I get something to eat, I'm starving," said Little Eagle.

"Don't eat too much, dinner will be ready in a couple hours," said Spirit Hawk.

"That is a neat place. I see why the Apache people liked it so much," said Lone Wolf.

"Yes it is son. It was also a safe haven for many years, until the Calvary found it," said Little Wolf.

"What was Sacred Wolf crying for," said Spirit Hawk.

"While we were digging, she was standing looking at the mountain, out of nowhere she started to cry. We ask her why and she said she could fill the sadness they felt," said Spirit Pony.

"That doesn't surprise me; she is a lot like her mom. The sensitive one," said Little Wolf.

"What does that mean," said Spirit Hawk.

"See, that's what I'm talking about. I would not have you any other way. Shows how girly you are," said Little Wolf.

"I love you too," said Spirit Hawk.

"Okay, I'm going to take a shower since all this mushy talk starts," said Lone Wolf.

"All of you need to take a shower, dinner will be ready soon," said Spirit Hawk.

"We will see you shortly mom, dad," said Spirit Wolf and Spirit Pony.

"Do you know how much I love you," said Spirit Hawk.

"Yes I do, that's why I'm the lucky one, I love you," said Little Wolf.

"Let's go fix dinner," said Spirit Hawk.

They fixed dinner, set around the dinner table and talked about Apache Leap and the adventure they had. One day they would take another journey there and to many other sacred sites to help protect what Mother Earth gave us all.

www.ingramcontent.com/pod-product-compliance
Lightning Source LLC
Chambersburg PA
CBHW071454030726
47593CB00003B/1007